CAT&CAT

ADVENTURES

The Goblet of Infinity

SUSIE YI

HARPER alley

An Imprint of HarperCollinsPublishers

Thank you to my family, Jack Gang, Yeon Yi, Man Jae Yi, and Heidi Yi, as well as my wonderful agent, Kathleen Ortiz, and the amazing team at HarperAlley who have made this book possible.

HarperAlley is an imprint of HarperCollins Publishers.
Cat & Cat Adventures: The Goblet of Infinity
Copyright © 2021 by Susie Yi.
All rights reserved. Manufactured in Italy.
No part of this book may be used or reproduced in any manner whatsoever without written permission except in the case of brief quotations embodied in critical articles and reviews. For information address HarperCollins Children's Books, a division of HarperCollins Publishers, 195 Broadway, New York, NY 10007.
www.harperalley.com
ISBN 978-0-06-308384-4 — ISBN 978-0-06-308383-7 (pbk.)

The artist used a computer, tablet, and the endless source of energy that only cats sitting in your lap can provide to create the digital illustrations for this book.

Typography by Susie Yi
22 23 24 25 26 RTLO 10 9 8 7 6 5 4 3 2 1

First Edition

CHAPTER ONE: Goblet

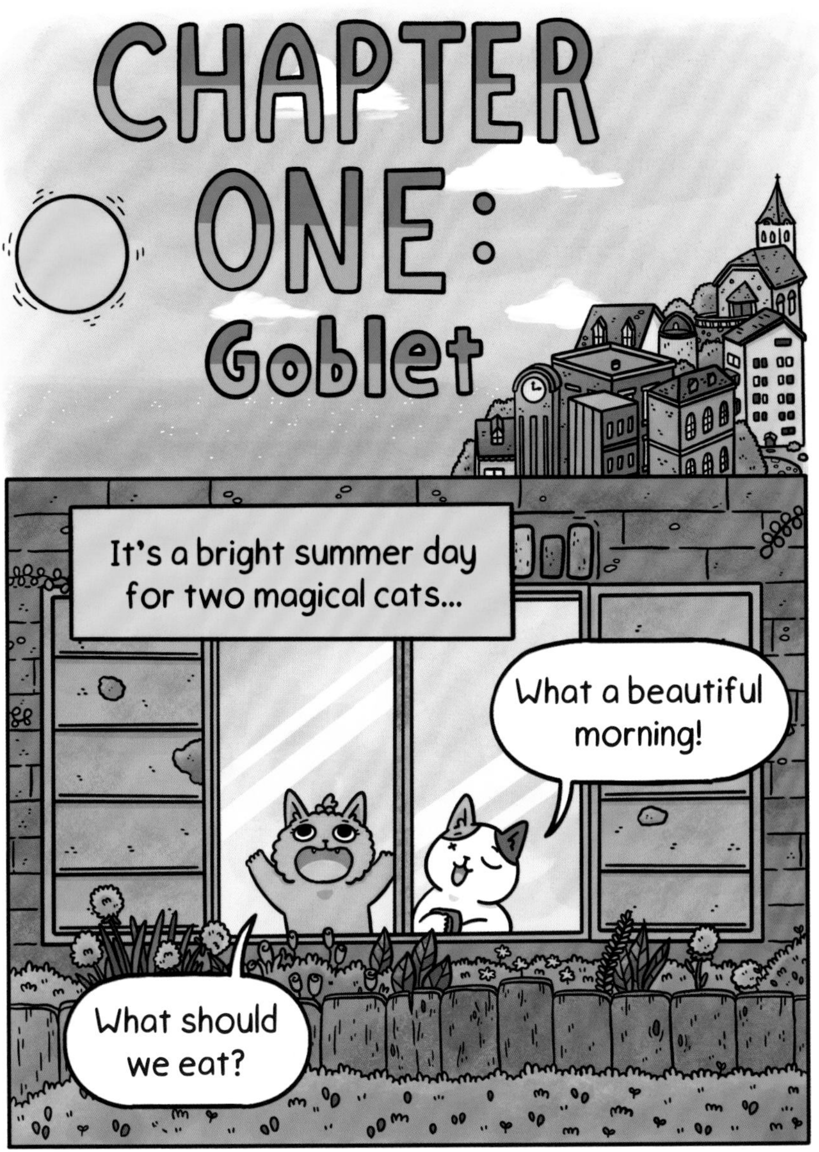
It's a bright summer day for two magical cats...
What a beautiful morning!
What should we eat?

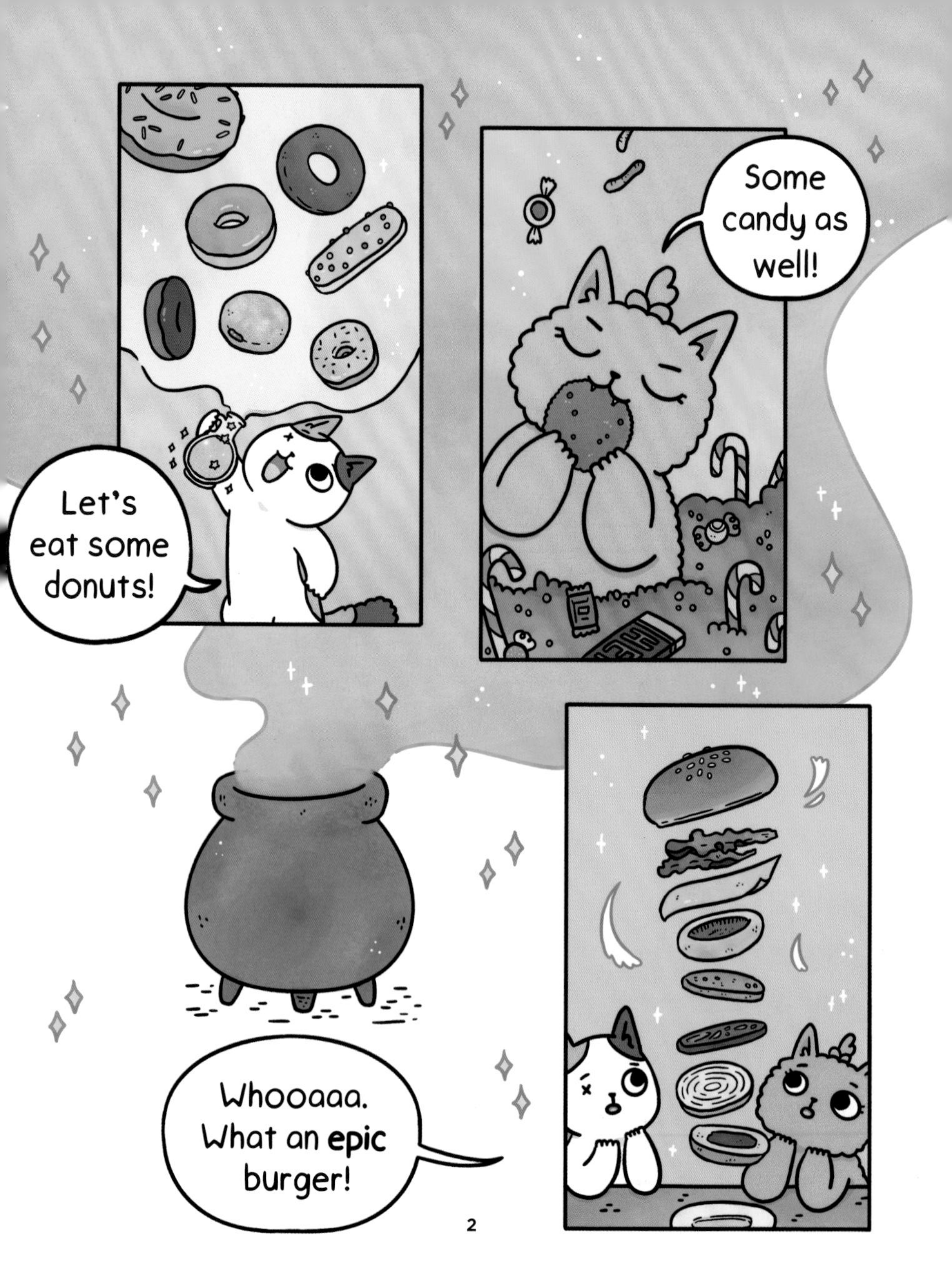

Let's eat some donuts!
Some candy as well!
Whooaaa. What an epic burger!

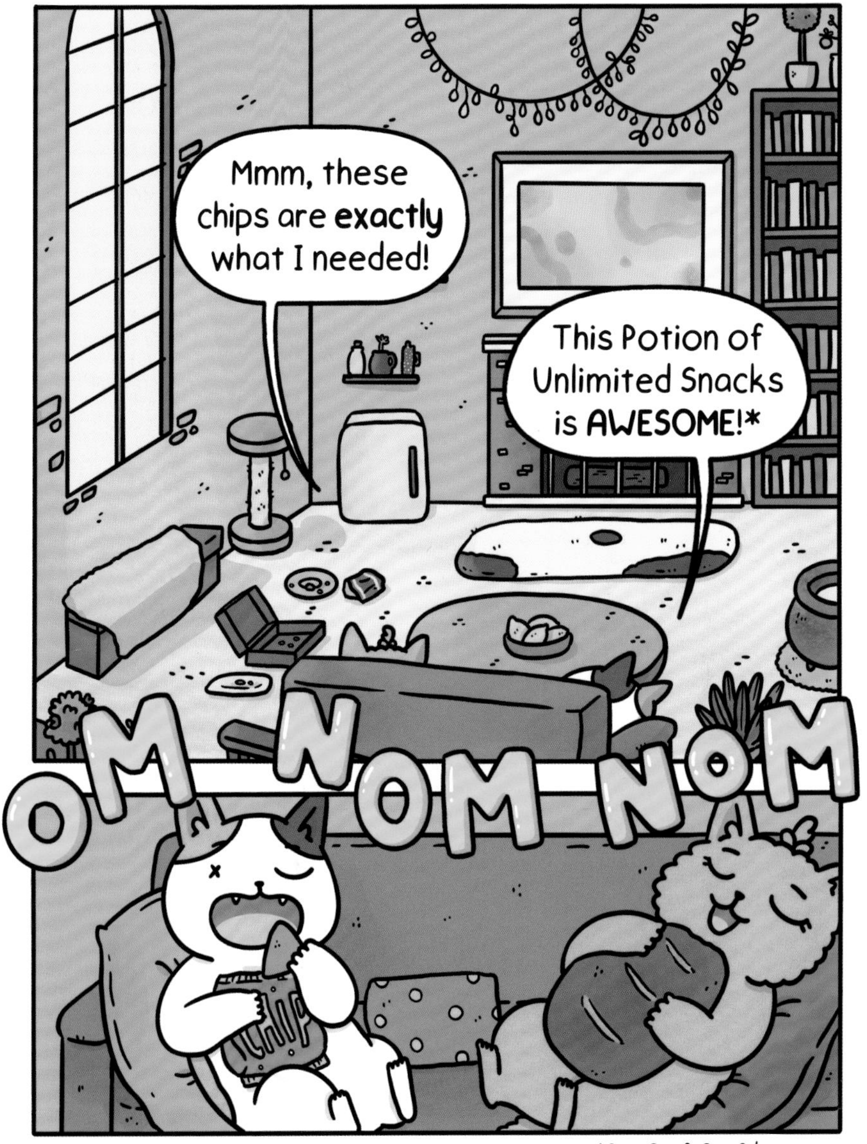
Mmm, these chips are **exactly** what I needed!
This Potion of Unlimited Snacks is **AWESOME!***
OM NOM NOM NOM NOM
CHIP

*See *Cat & Cat Adventures: The Quest for Snacks*

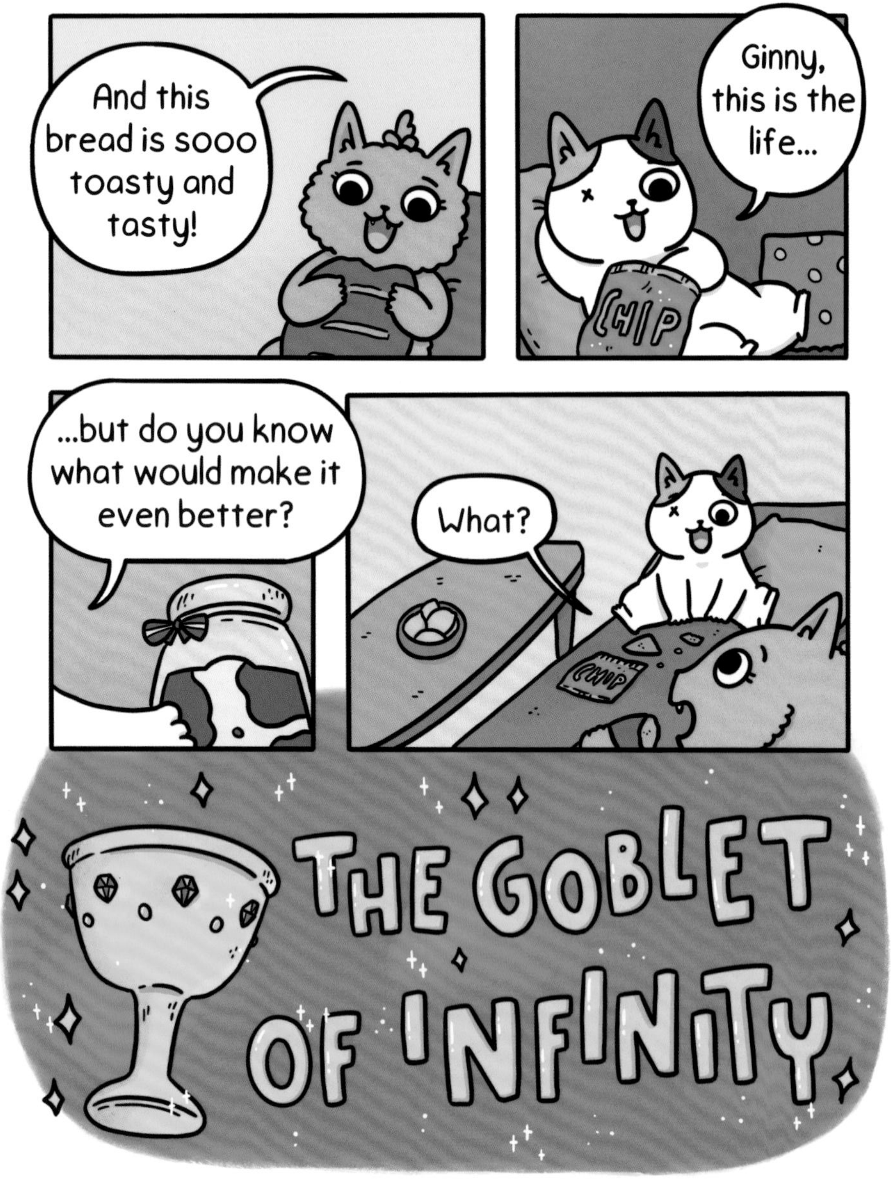
And this bread is sooo toasty and tasty!
Ginny, this is the life...
CHIP
...but do you know what would make it even better?
What?
CHIP
THE GOBLET OF INFINITY

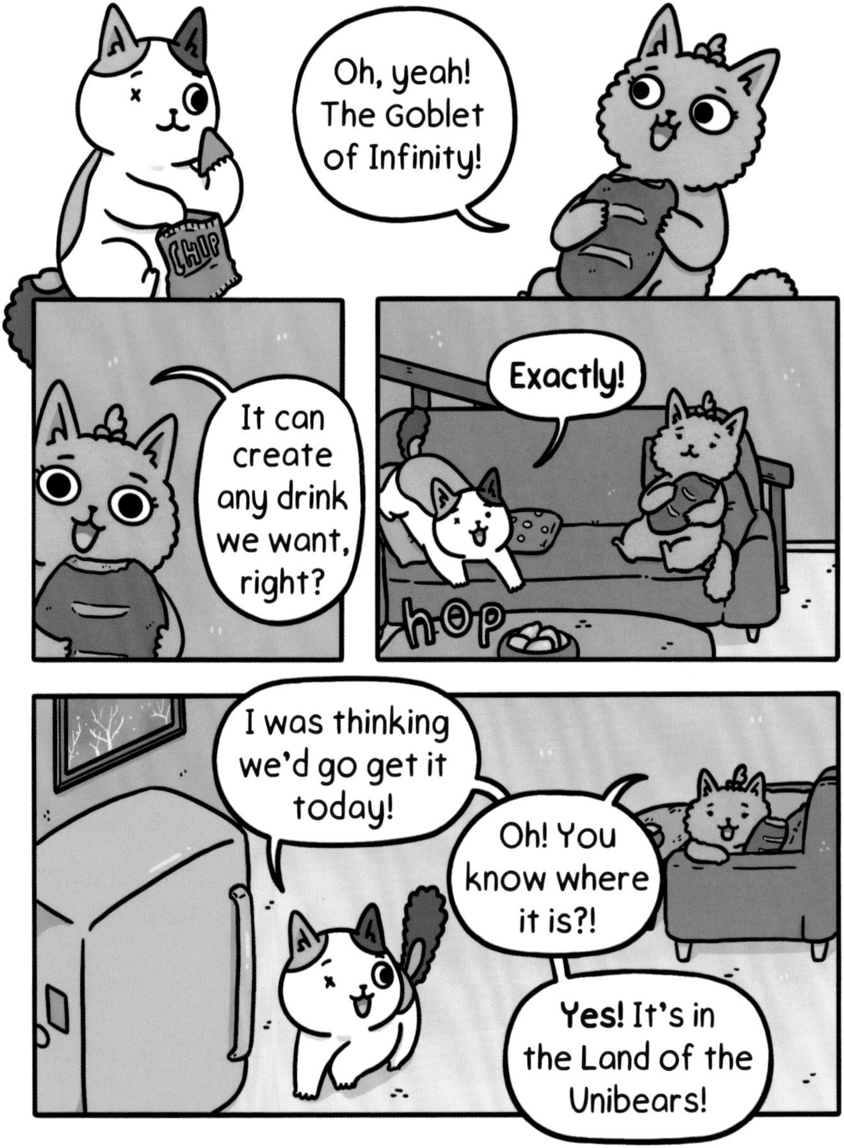
Oh, yeah! The Goblet of Infinity!
CHIP
It can create any drink we want, right?
Exactly!
hop
I was thinking we'd go get it today!
Oh! You know where it is?!
Yes! It's in the Land of the Unibears!

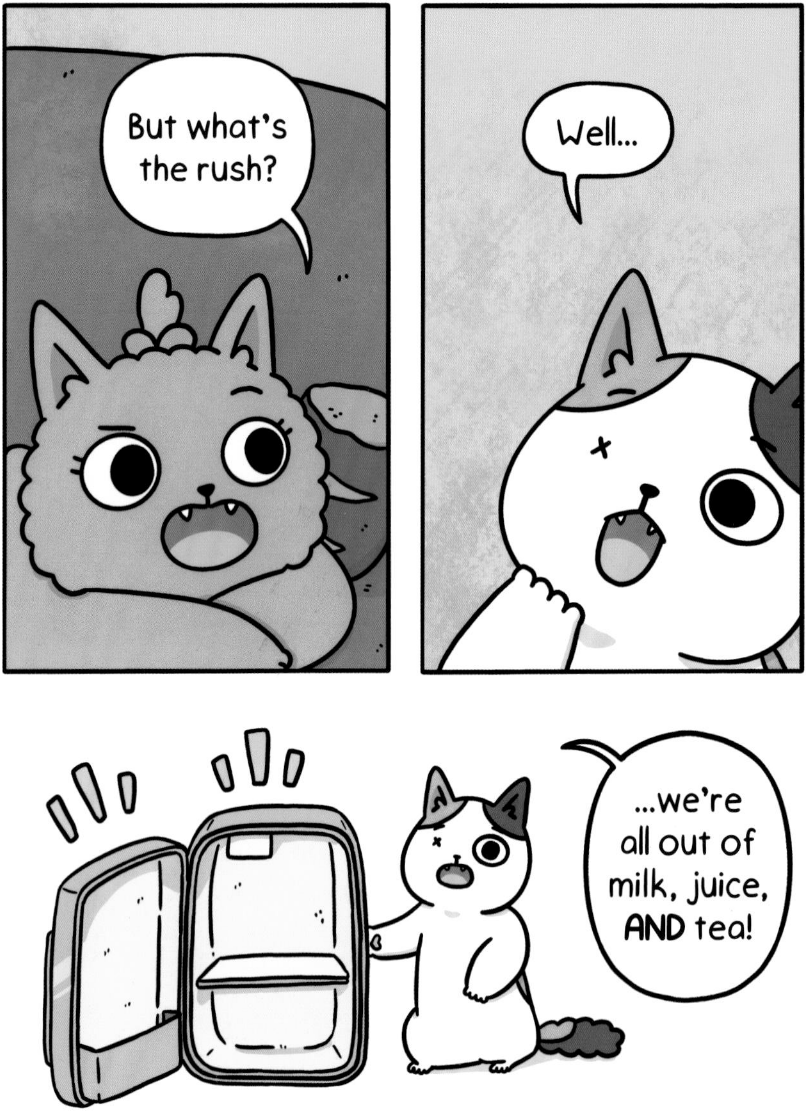
But what's the rush?
Well...
...we're all out of milk, juice, AND tea!

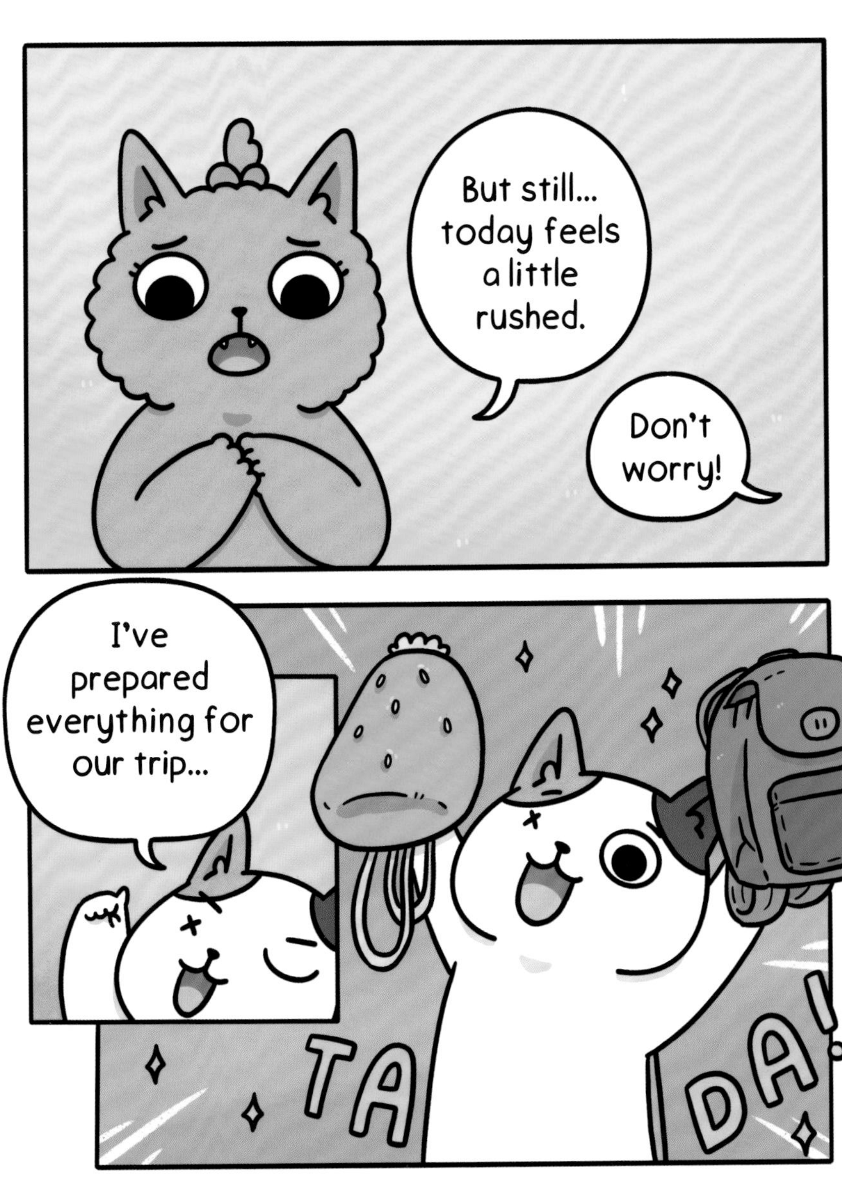
But still... today feels a little rushed.
Don't worry!
I've prepared everything for our trip...
TA DA!

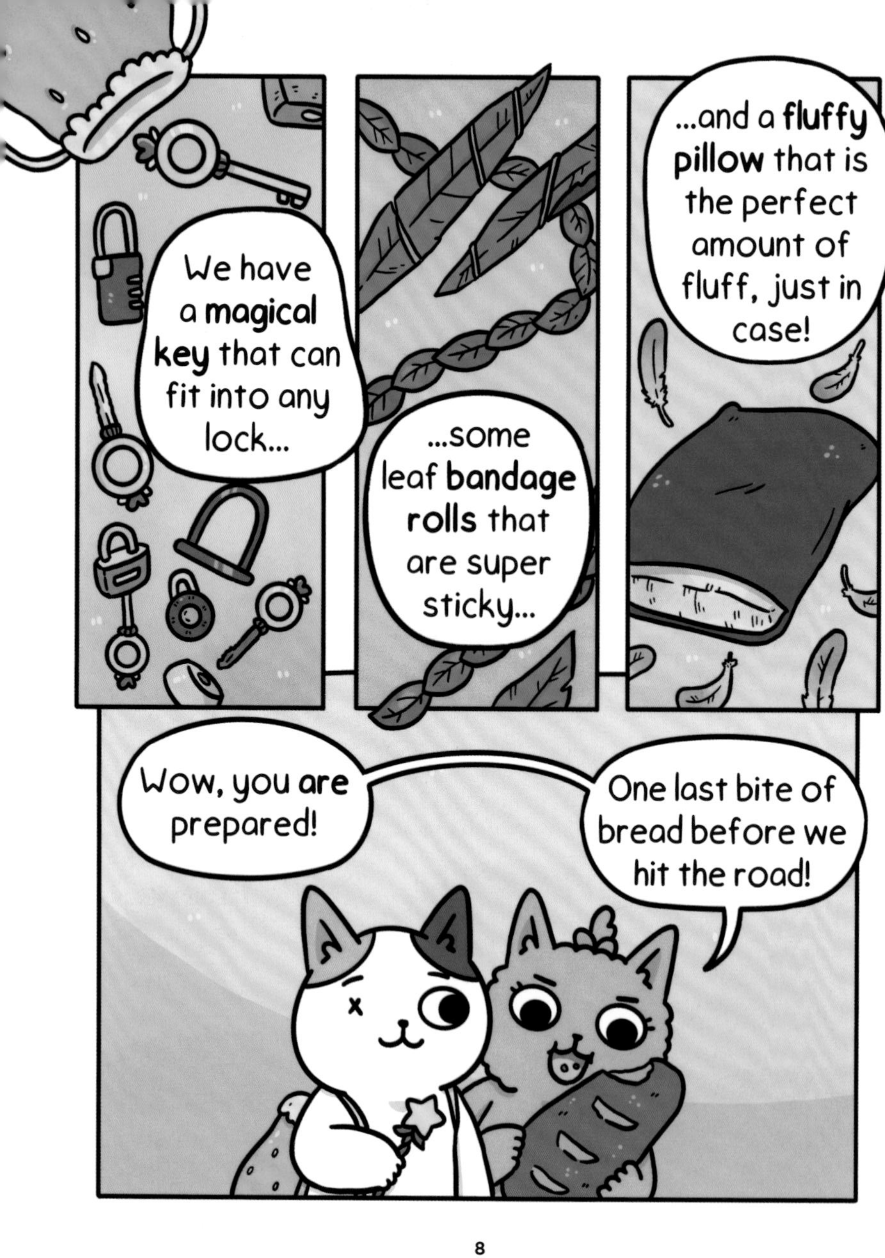
We have a **magical key** that can fit into any lock...
...some leaf **bandage rolls** that are super sticky...
...and a **fluffy pillow** that is the perfect amount of fluff, just in case!
Wow, you **are** prepared!
One last bite of bread before we hit the road!

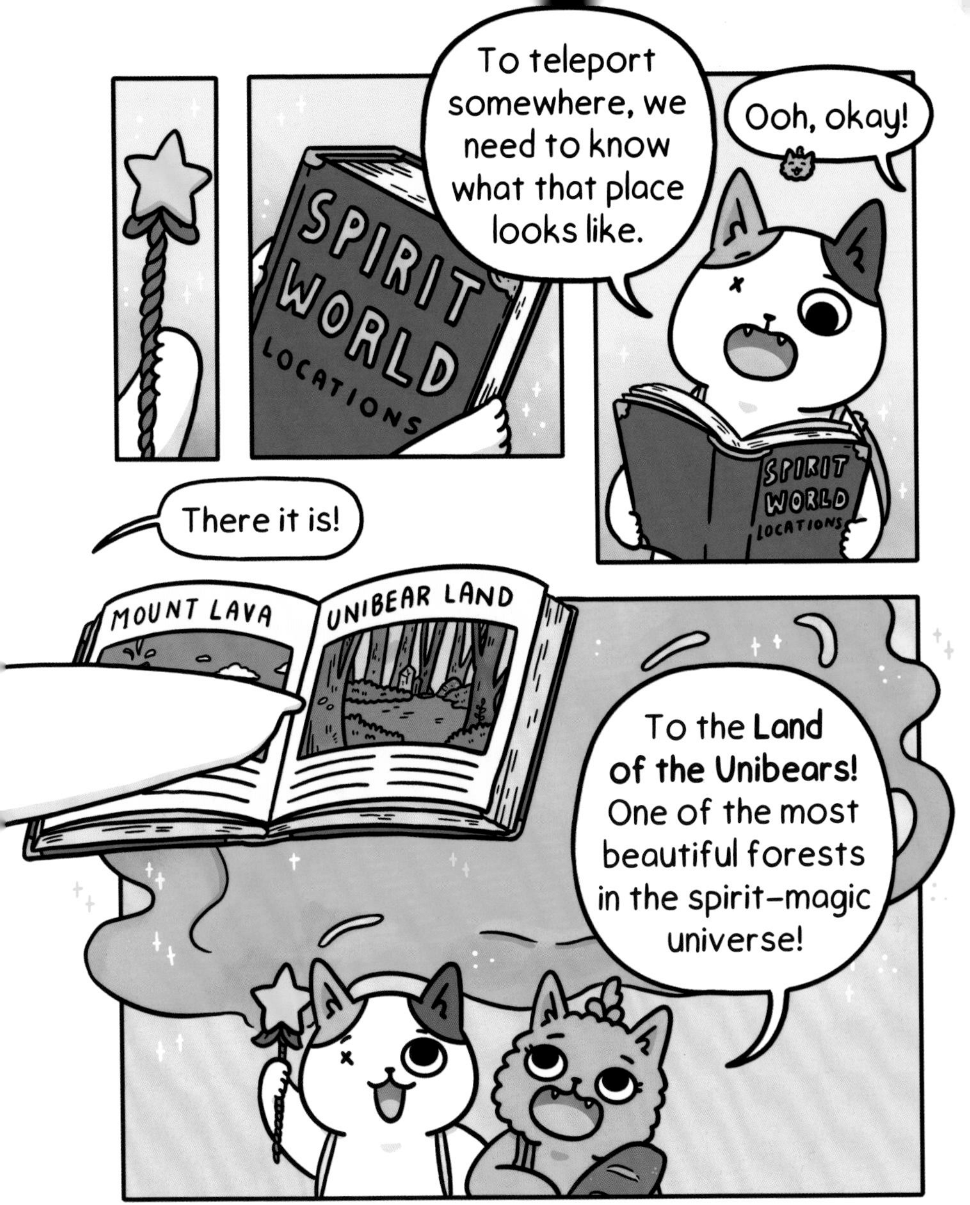

SPIRIT WORLD LOCATIONS
To teleport somewhere, we need to know what that place looks like.
Ooh, okay!
SPIRIT WORLD LOCATIONS
There it is!
MOUNT LAVA
UNIBEAR LAND
To the **Land of the Unibears!** One of the most beautiful forests in the spirit-magic universe!

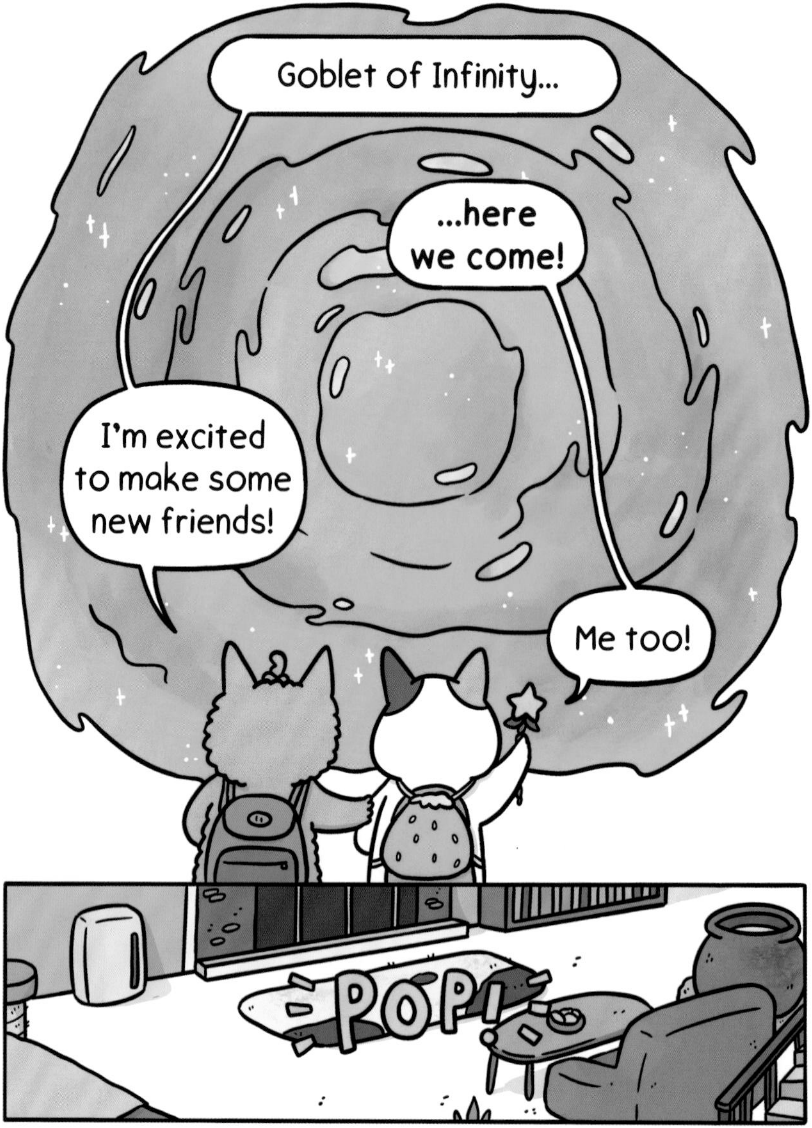
Goblet of Infinity...
...here we come!
I'm excited to make some new friends!
Me too!
POP!

WHEE!

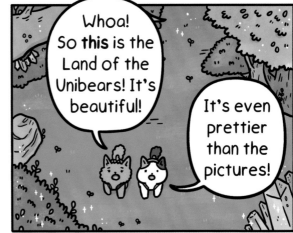

Whoa! So **this** is the Land of the Unibears! It's beautiful!

It's even prettier than the pictures!

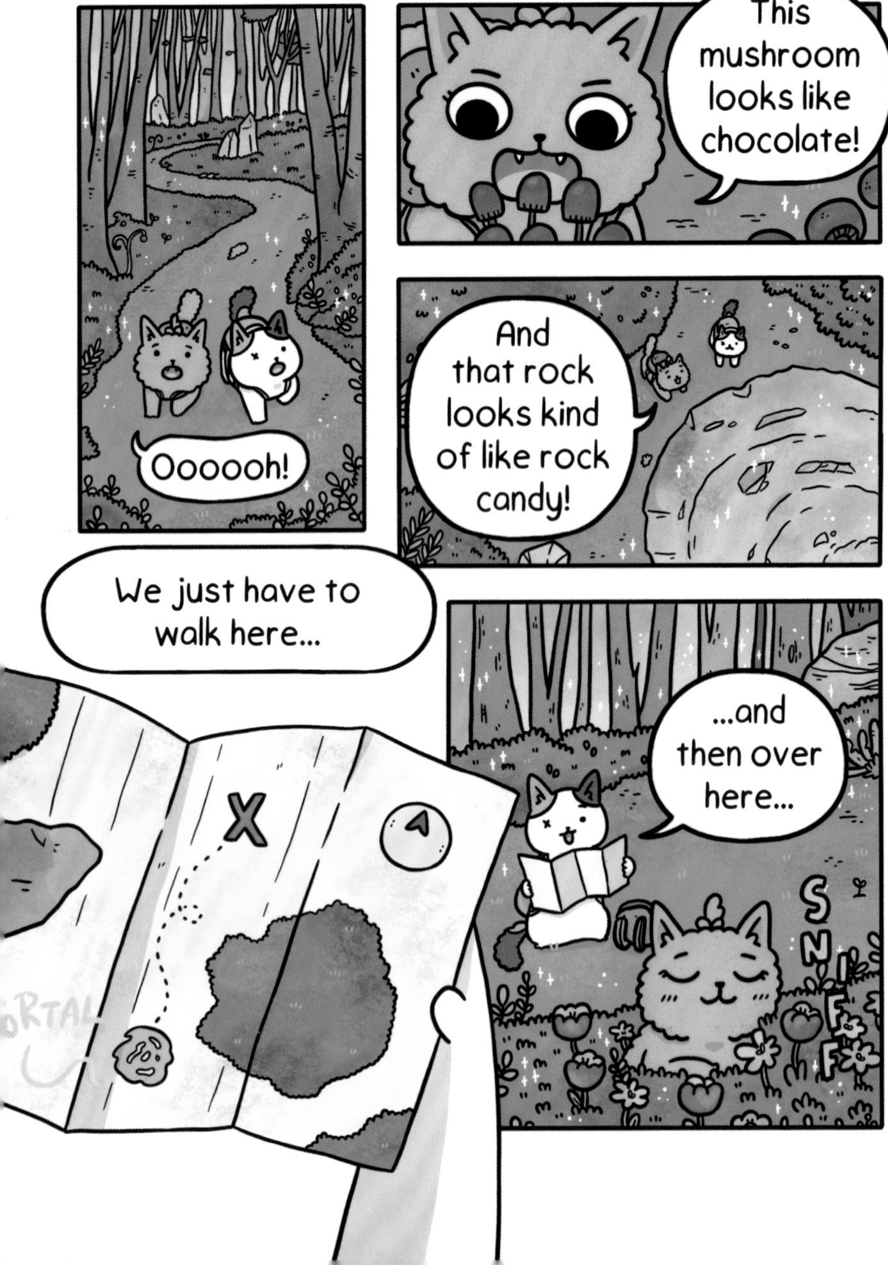
Oooooh!
This mushroom looks like chocolate!
And that rock looks kind of like rock candy!
We just have to walk here...
X
ORTAL
...and then over here...
SNIFF

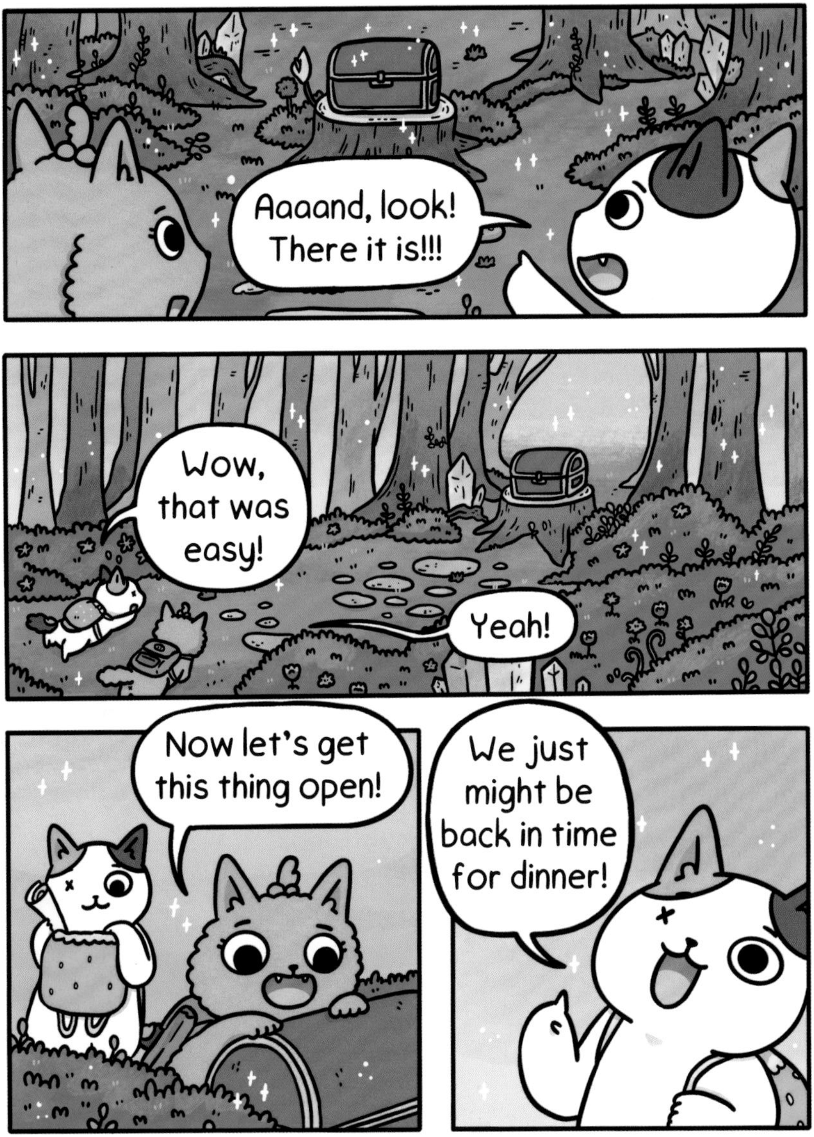
Aaaand, look! There it is!!!
Wow, that was easy!
Yeah!
Now let's get this thing open!
We just might be back in time for dinner!

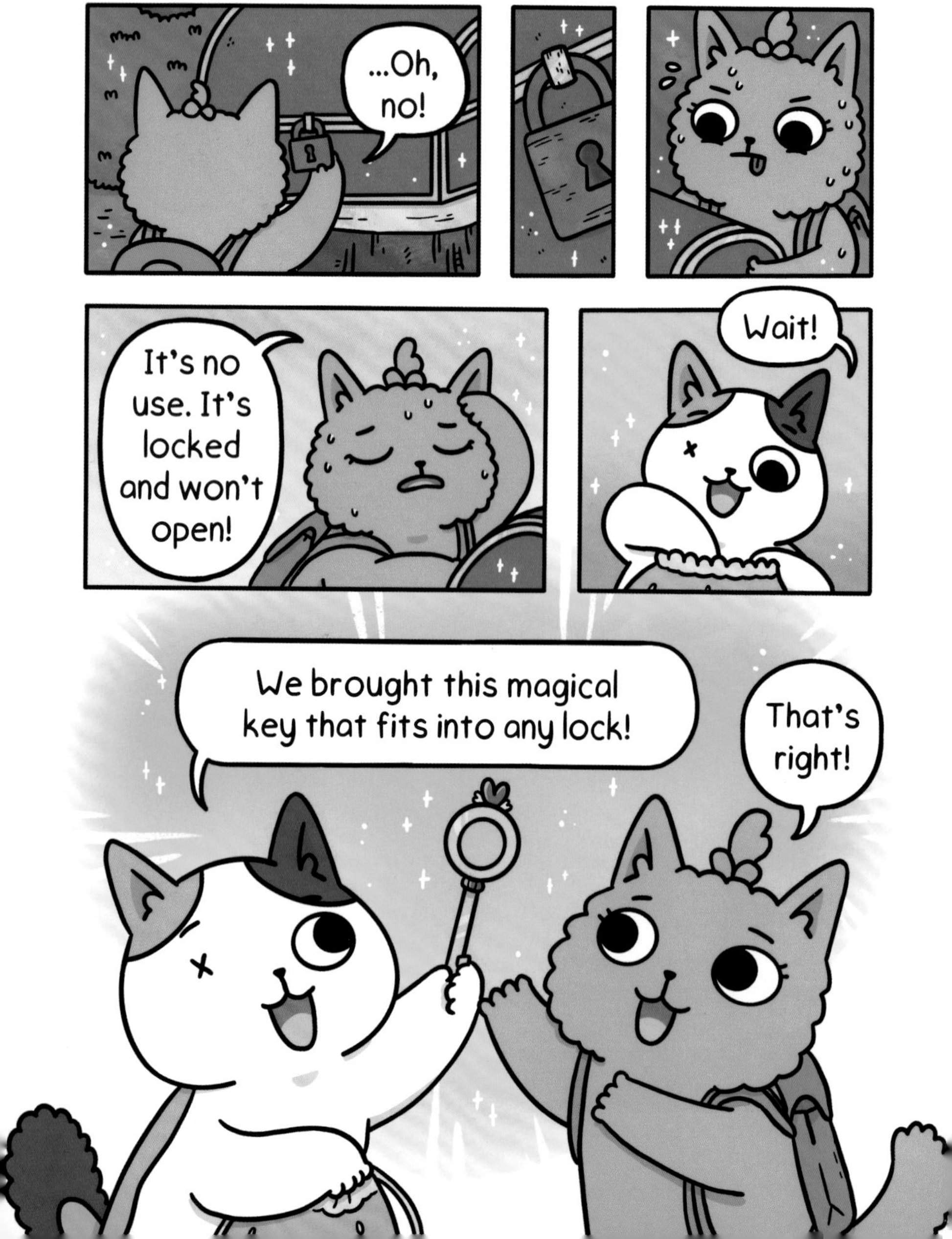
...Oh, no!
It's no use. It's locked and won't open!
Wait!
We brought this magical key that fits into any lock!
That's right!

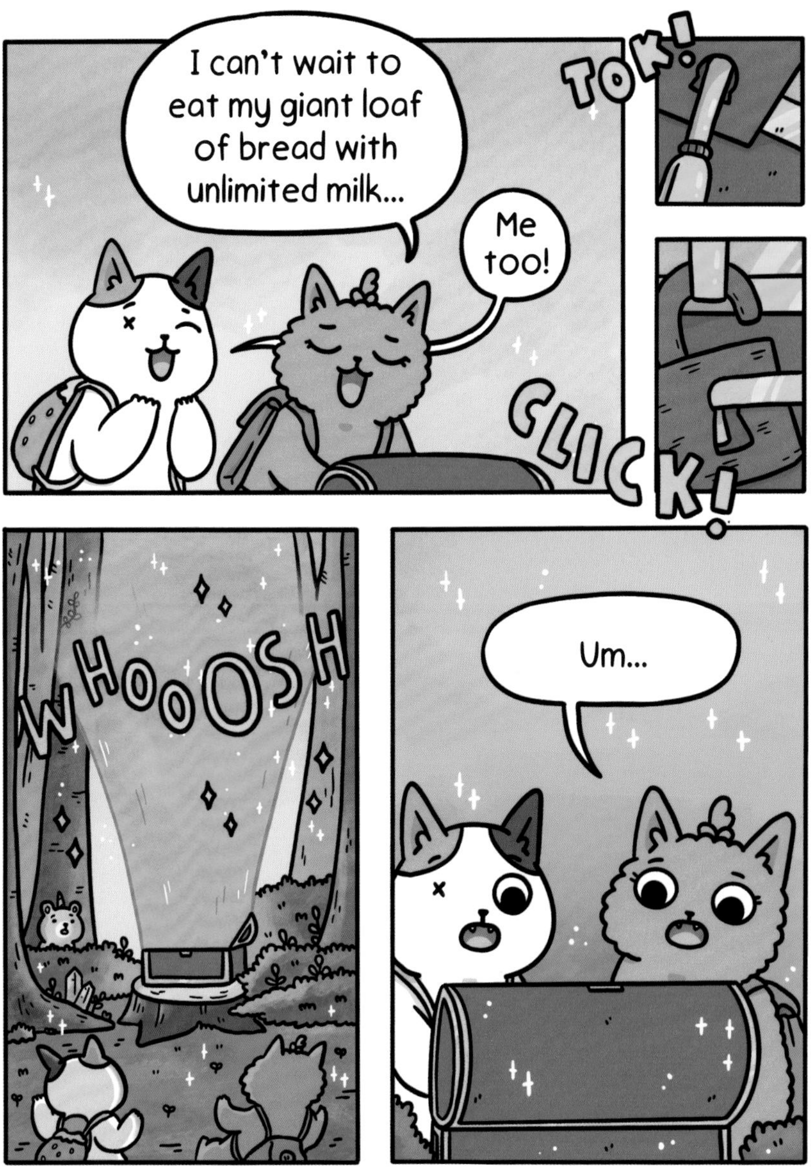
I can't wait to eat my giant loaf of bread with unlimited milk...
Me too!
TOK!
CLICK!
WHOOOSH
Um...

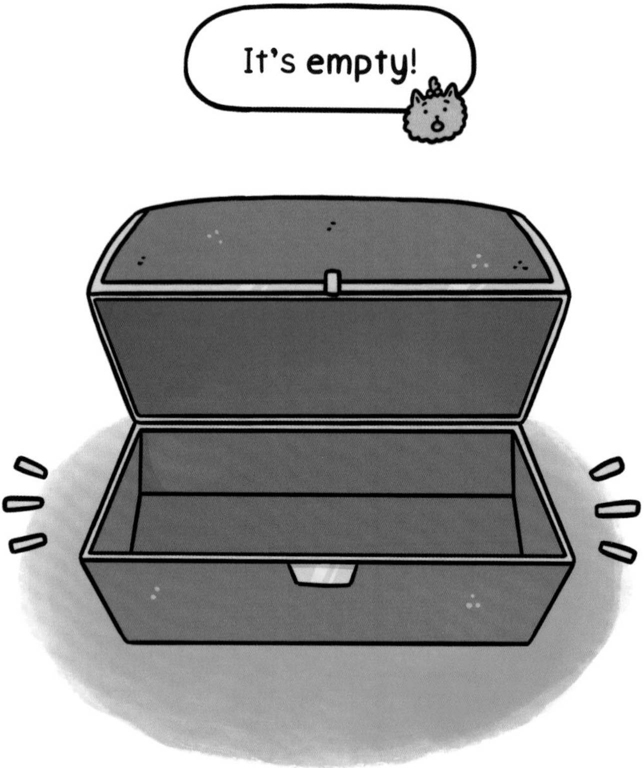
It's empty!

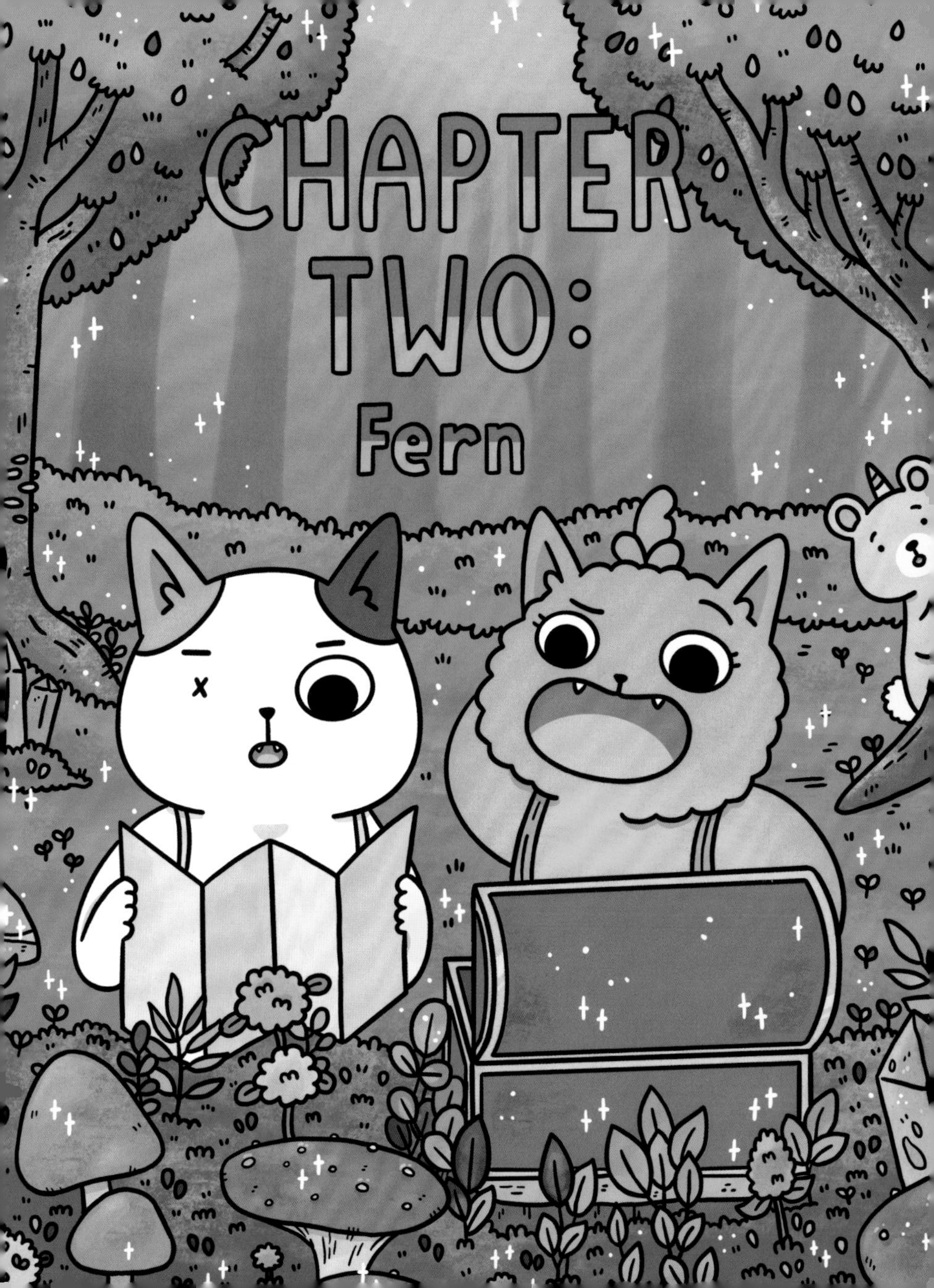
CHAPTER
TWO:
Fern

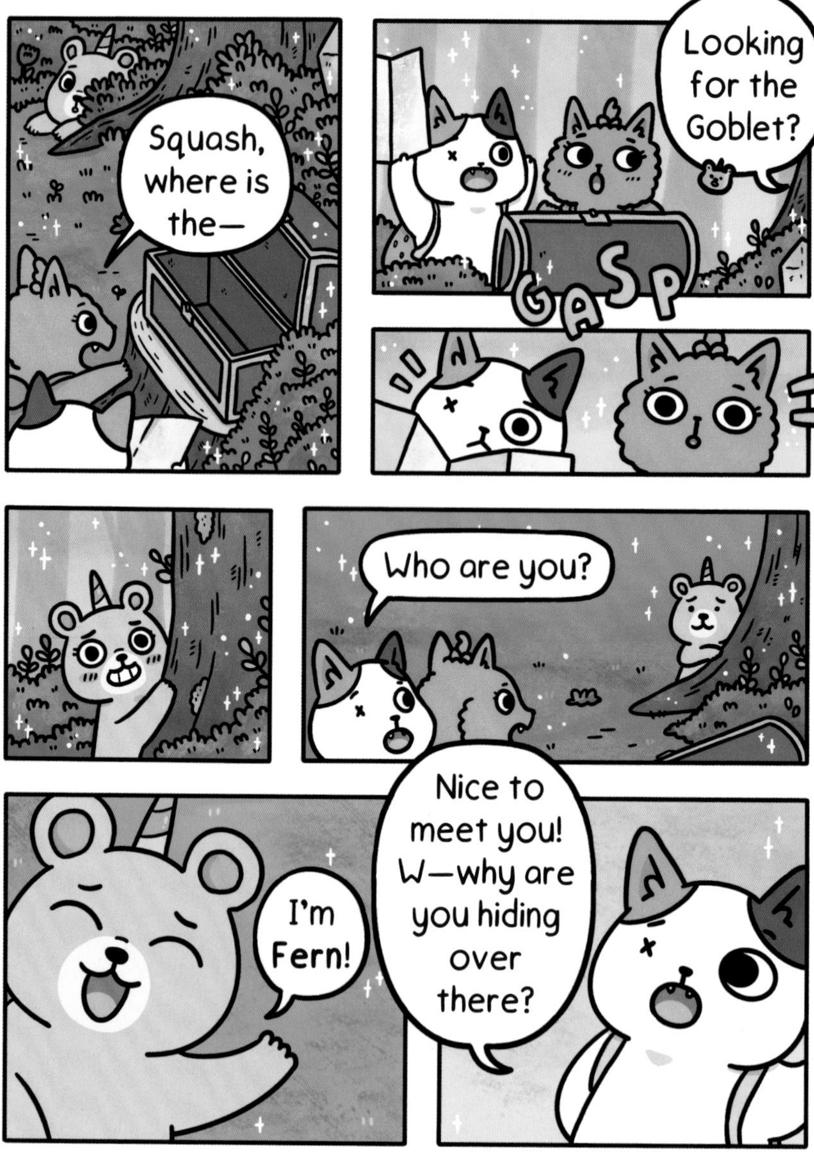
Squash, where is the—
Looking for the Goblet?
GASP
Who are you?
I'm Fern!
Nice to meet you! W—why are you hiding over there?

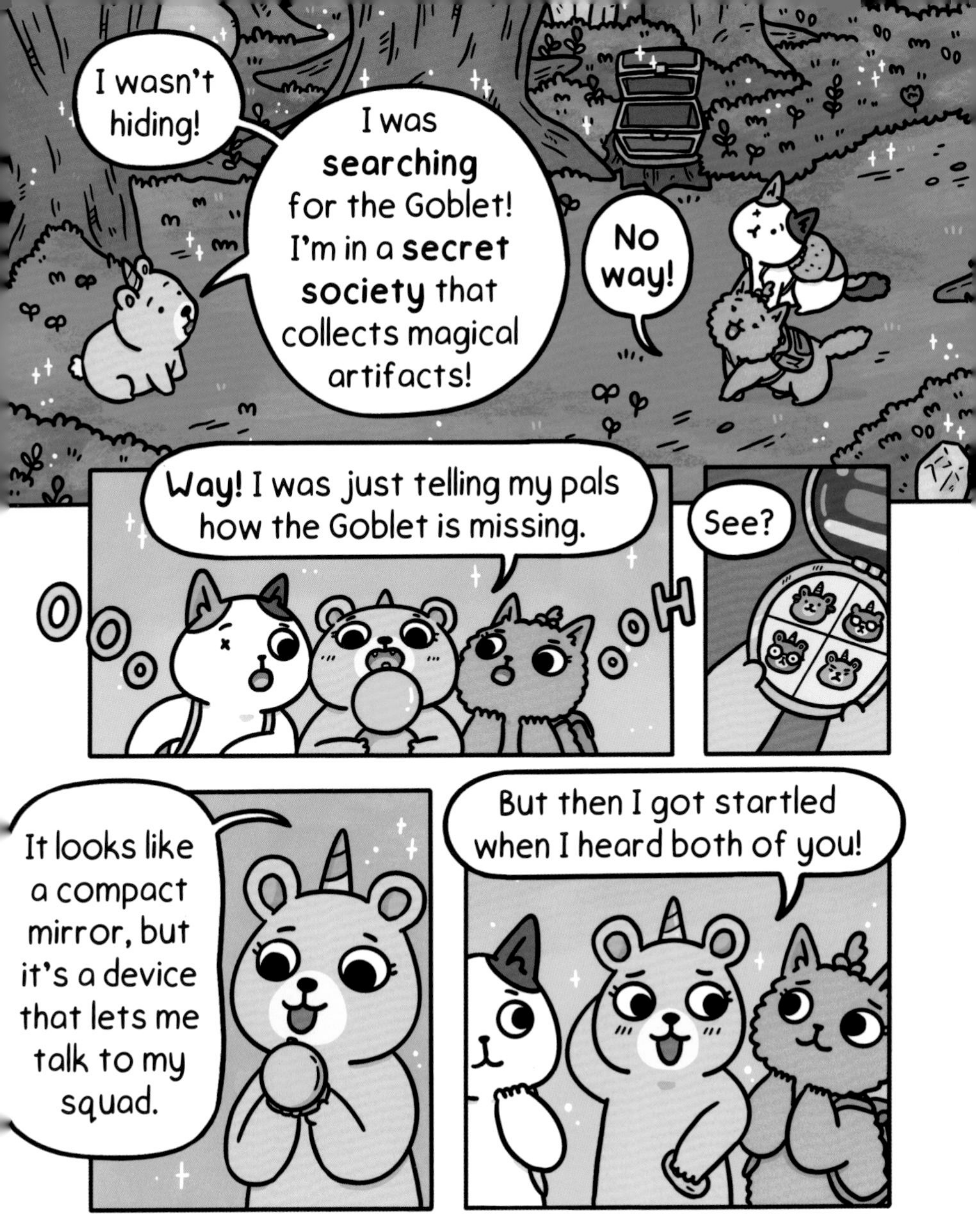
I wasn't hiding!
I was **searching** for the Goblet! I'm in a **secret society** that collects magical artifacts!
No way!
Way! I was just telling my pals how the Goblet is missing.
OOOOOOOH
See?
It looks like a compact mirror, but it's a device that lets me talk to my squad.
But then I got startled when I heard both of you!

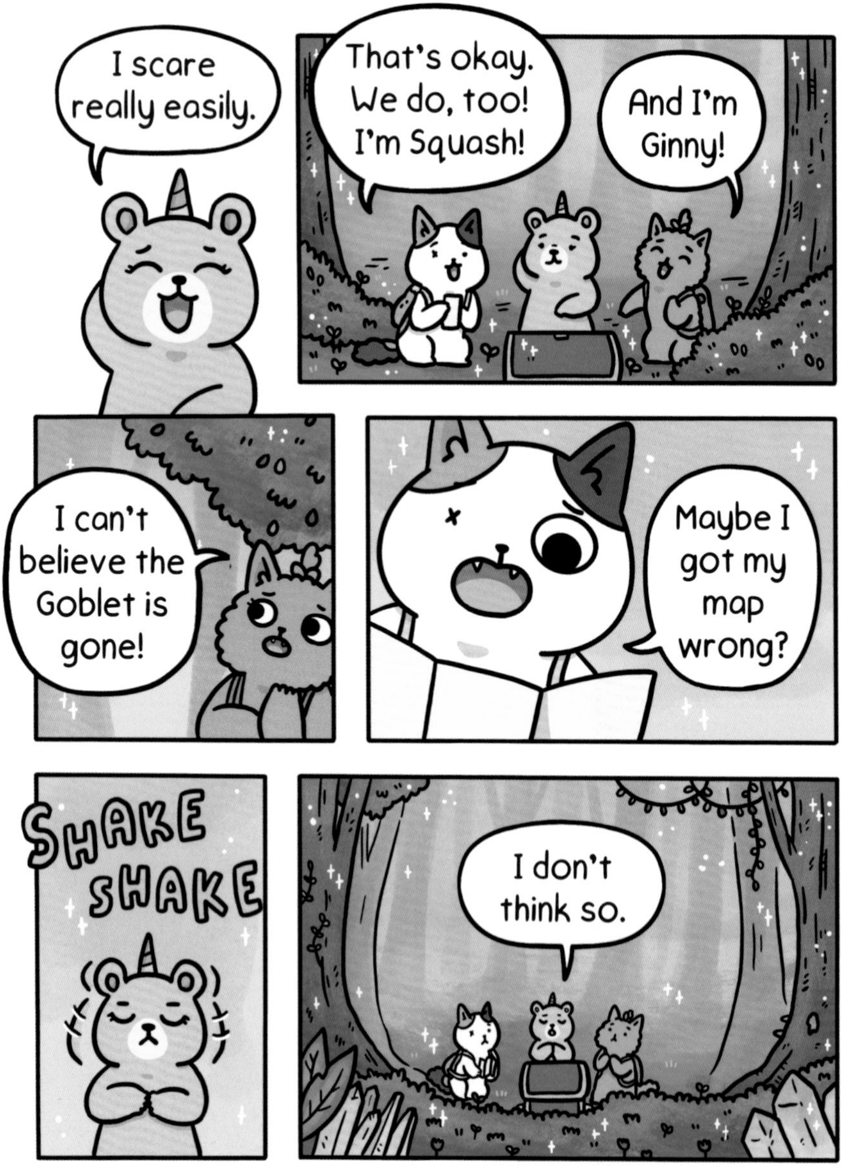
I scare really easily.
That's okay. We do, too! I'm Squash!
And I'm Ginny!
I can't believe the Goblet is gone!
Maybe I got my map wrong?
SHAKE SHAKE
I don't think so.

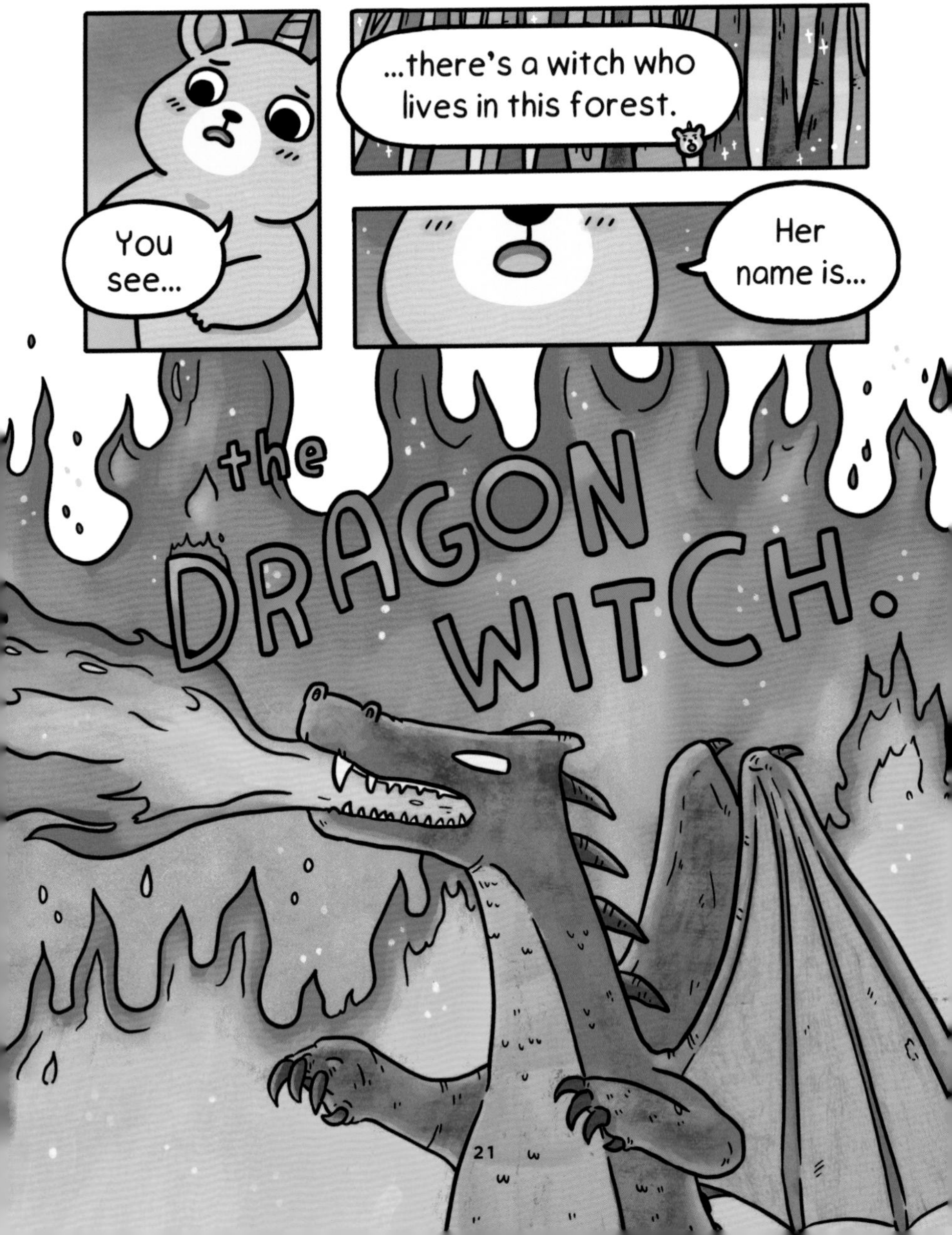
You see...
...there's a witch who lives in this forest.
Her name is...
the DRAGON WITCH.

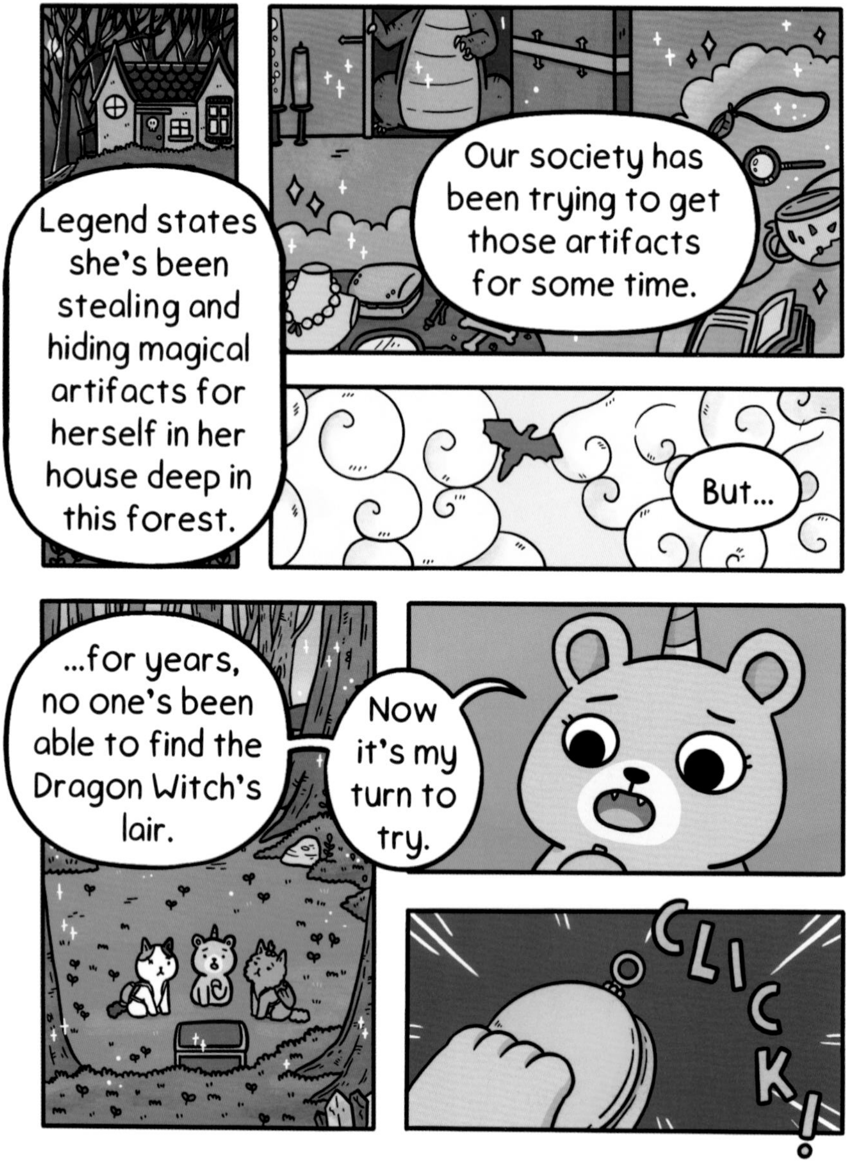
Legend states she's been stealing and hiding magical artifacts for herself in her house deep in this forest.
Our society has been trying to get those artifacts for some time.
But...
...for years, no one's been able to find the Dragon Witch's lair.
Now it's my turn to try.
CLICK!

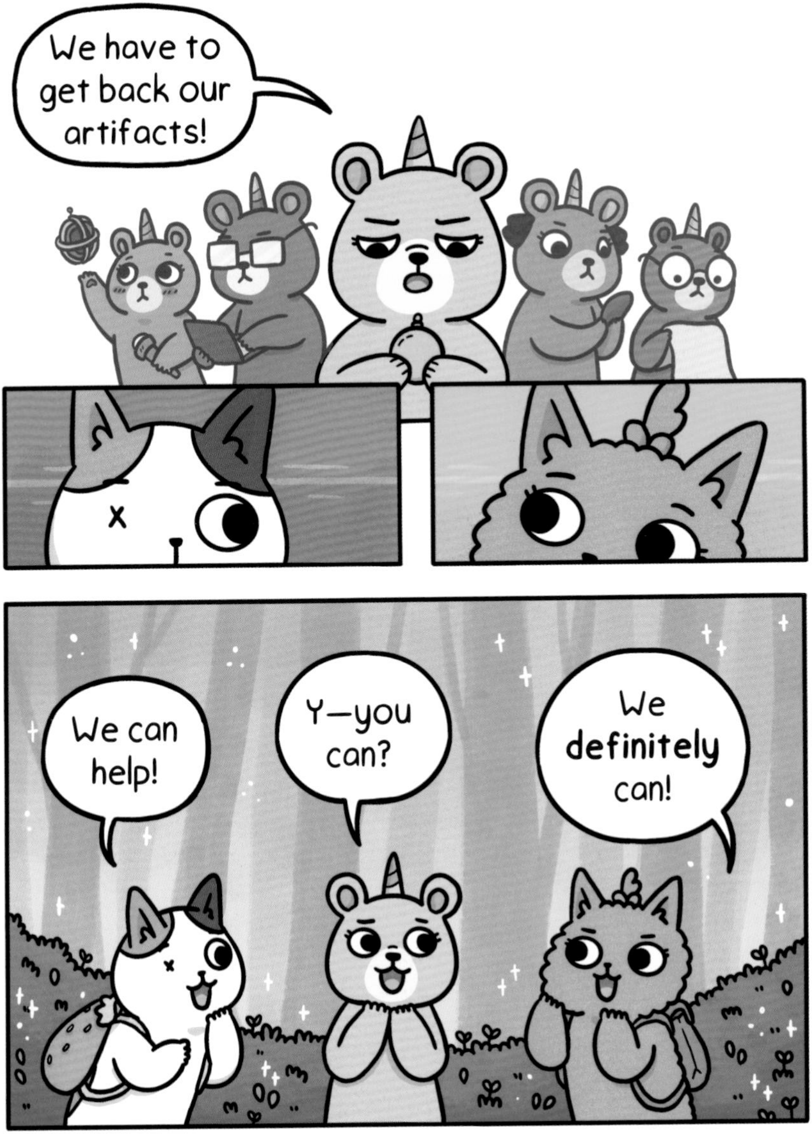
We have to get back our artifacts!
We can help!
Y—you can?
We **definitely** can!

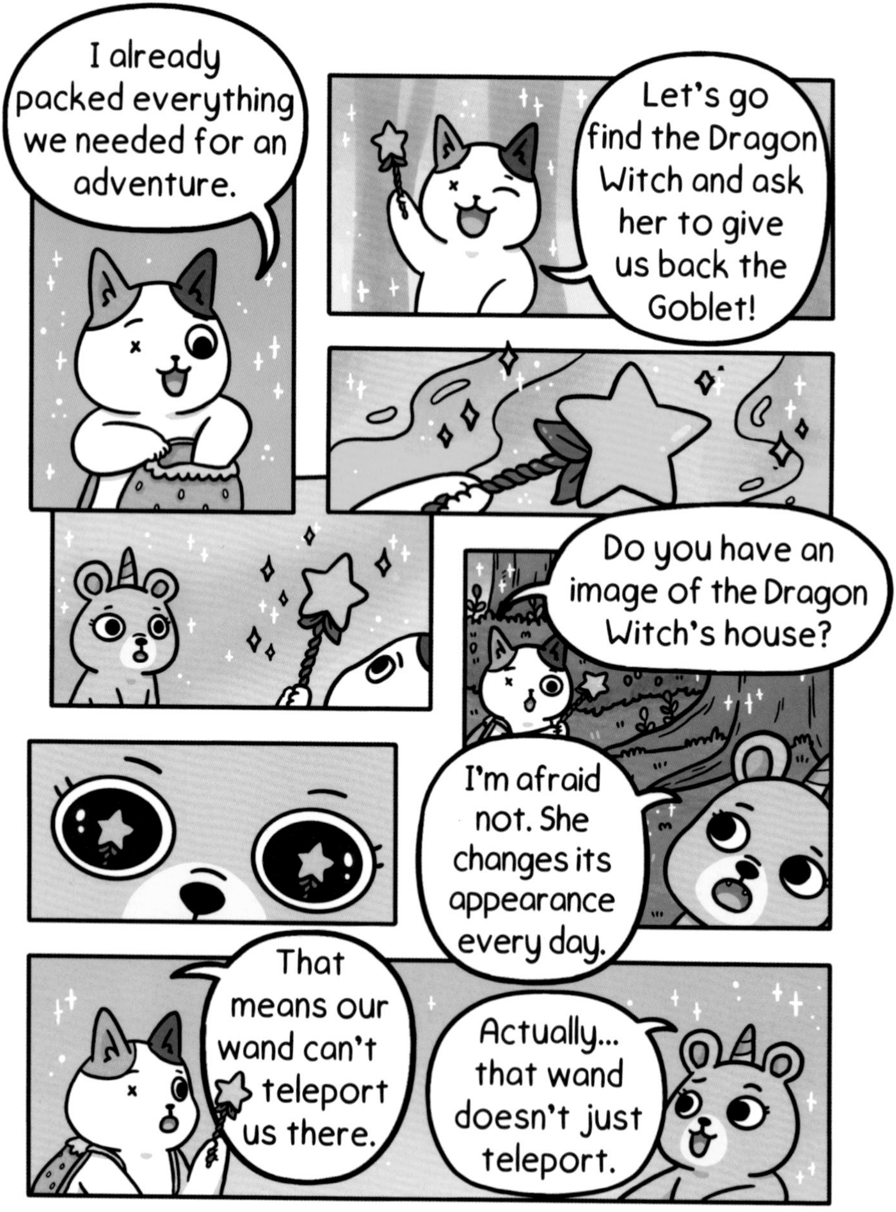
I already packed everything we needed for an adventure.
Let's go find the Dragon Witch and ask her to give us back the Goblet!
Do you have an image of the Dragon Witch's house?
I'm afraid not. She changes its appearance every day.
That means our wand can't teleport us there.
Actually... that wand doesn't just teleport.

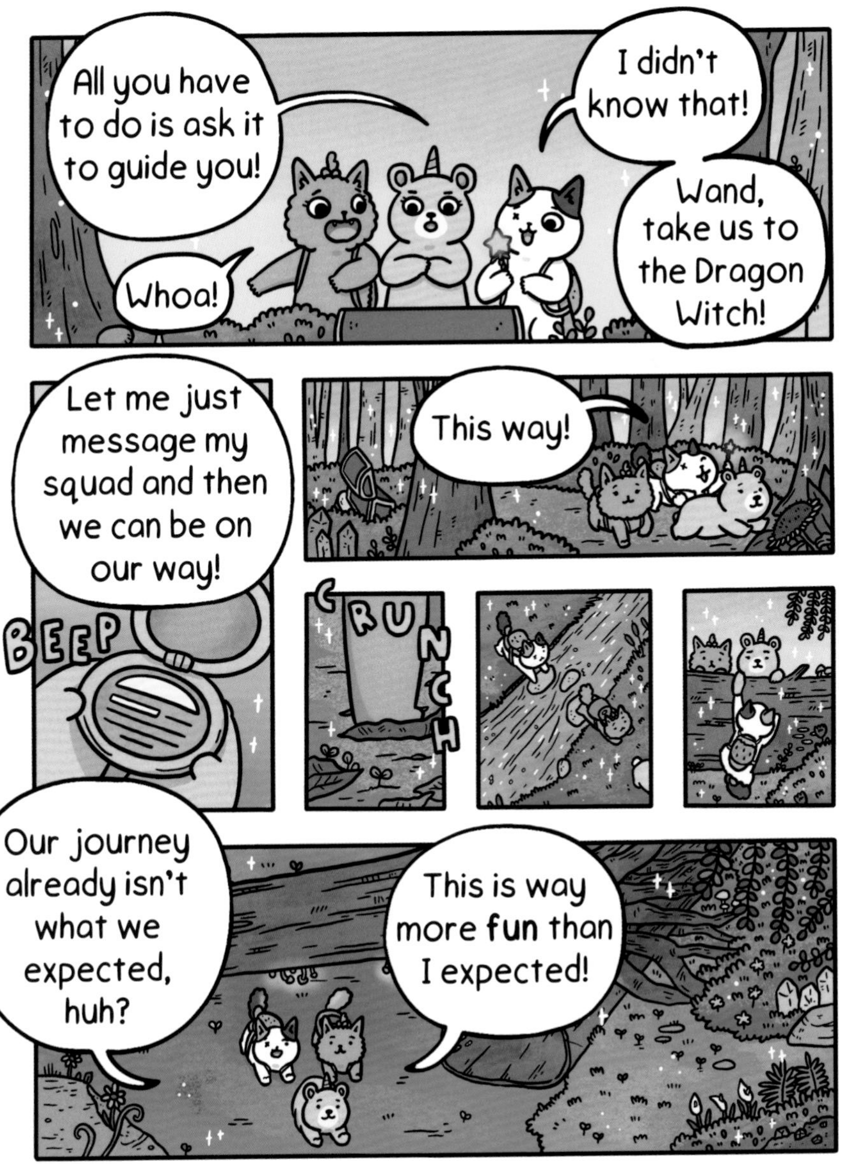
All you have to do is ask it to guide you!
Whoa!
I didn't know that!
Wand, take us to the Dragon Witch!
Let me just message my squad and then we can be on our way!
BEEP
This way!
CRUNCH
Our journey already isn't what we expected, huh?
This is way more **fun** than I expected!

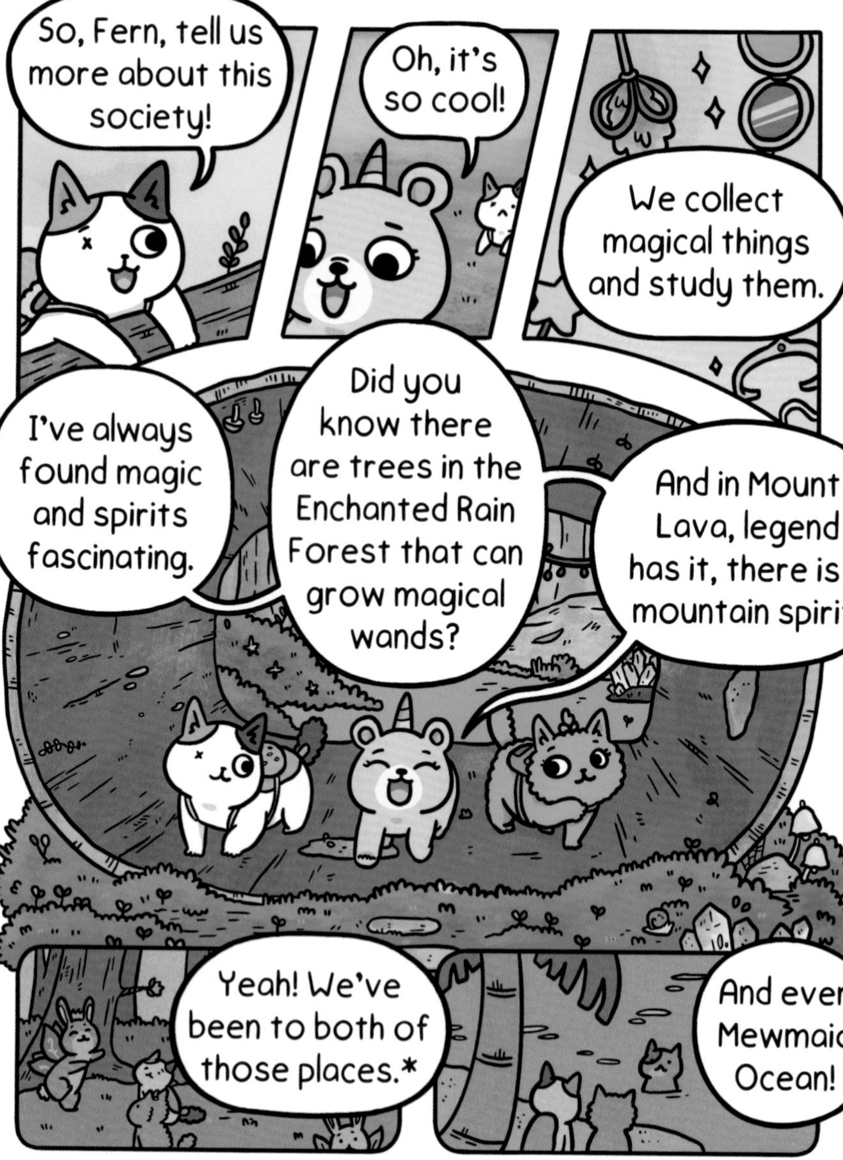
So, Fern, tell us more about this society!
Oh, it's so cool!
We collect magical things and study them.
I've always found magic and spirits fascinating.
Did you know there are trees in the Enchanted Rain Forest that can grow magical wands?
And in Mount Lava, legend has it, there is a mountain spirit!
Yeah! We've been to both of those places.*
And even Mewmaid Ocean!

*See *Cat & Cat Adventures: The Quest for Snacks*

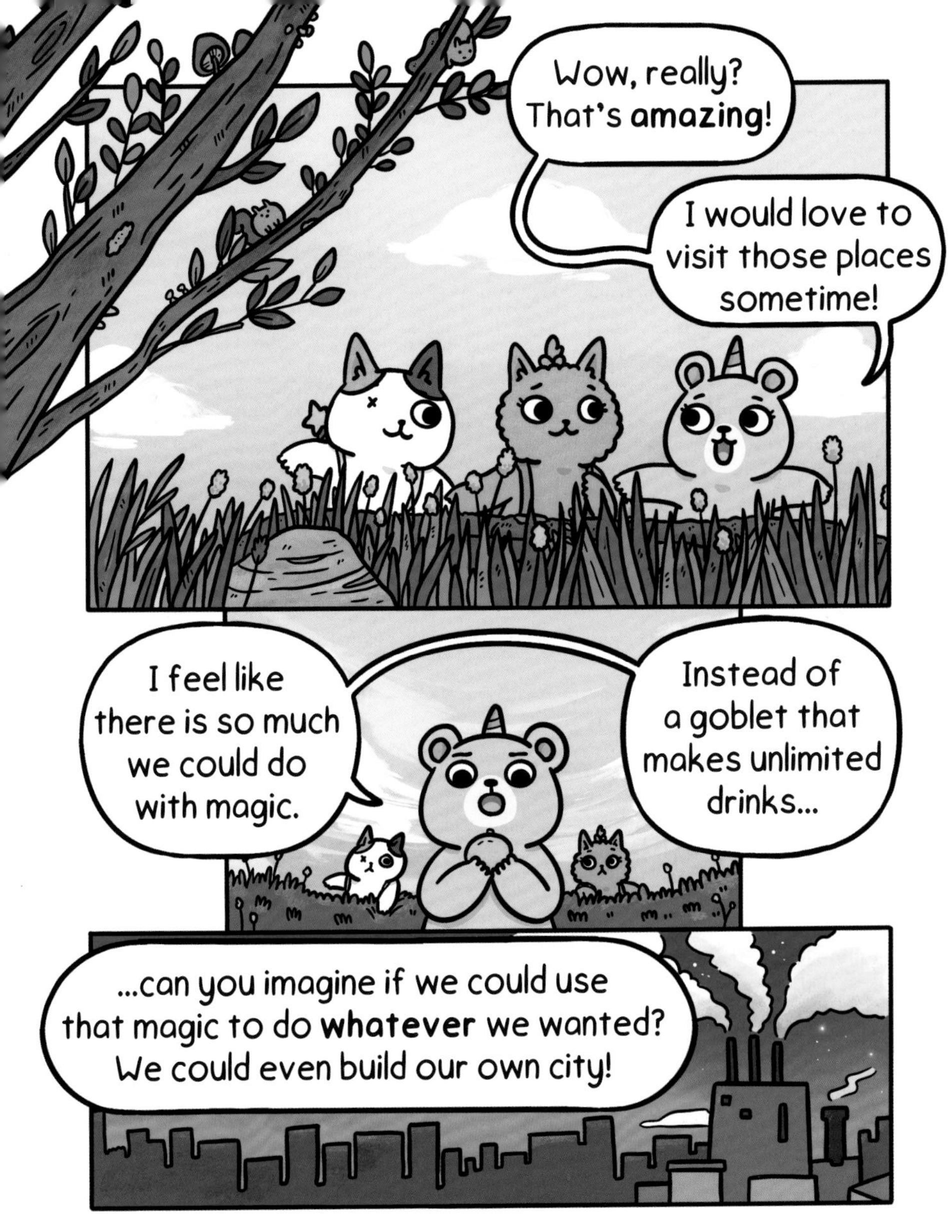

Wow, really? That's **amazing**!
I would love to visit those places sometime!
I feel like there is so much we could do with magic.
Instead of a goblet that makes unlimited drinks...
...can you imagine if we could use that magic to do **whatever** we wanted? We could even build our own city!

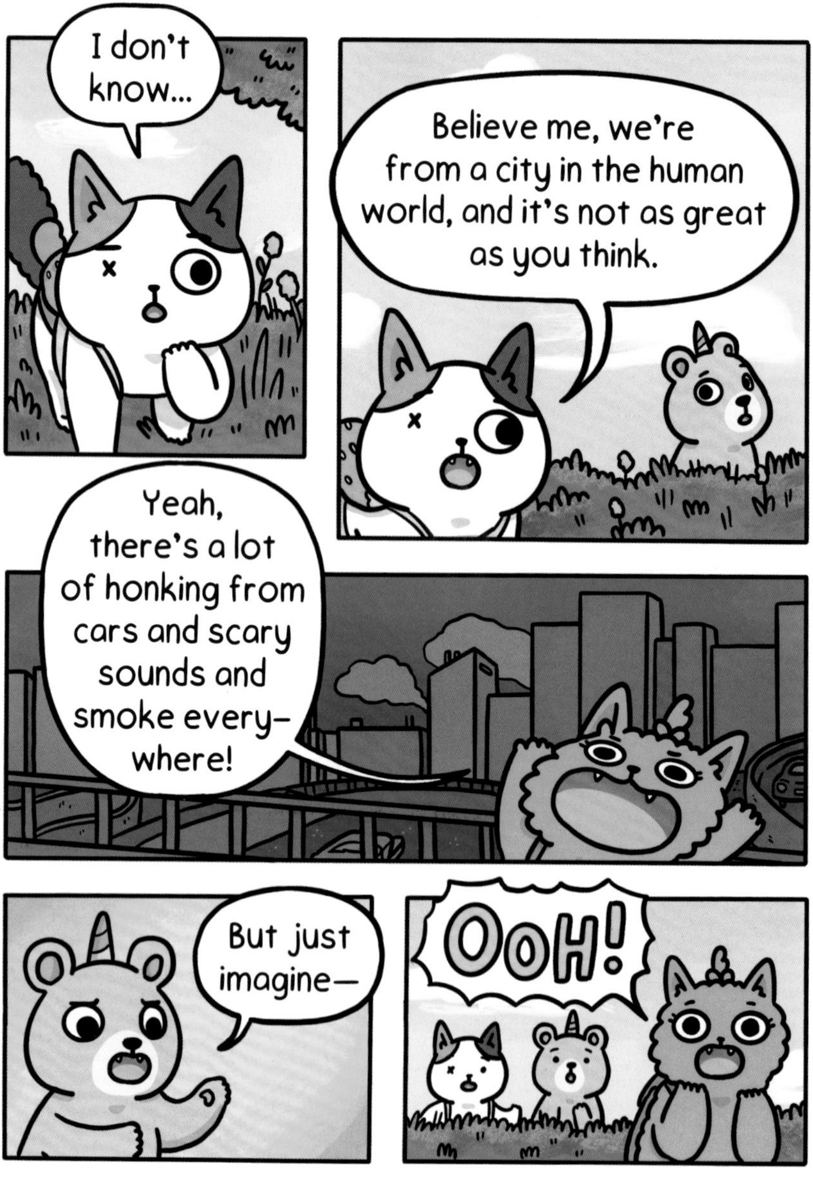
I don't know...
Believe me, we're from a city in the human world, and it's not as great as you think.
Yeah, there's a lot of honking from cars and scary sounds and smoke every-where!
But just imagine—
OOH!

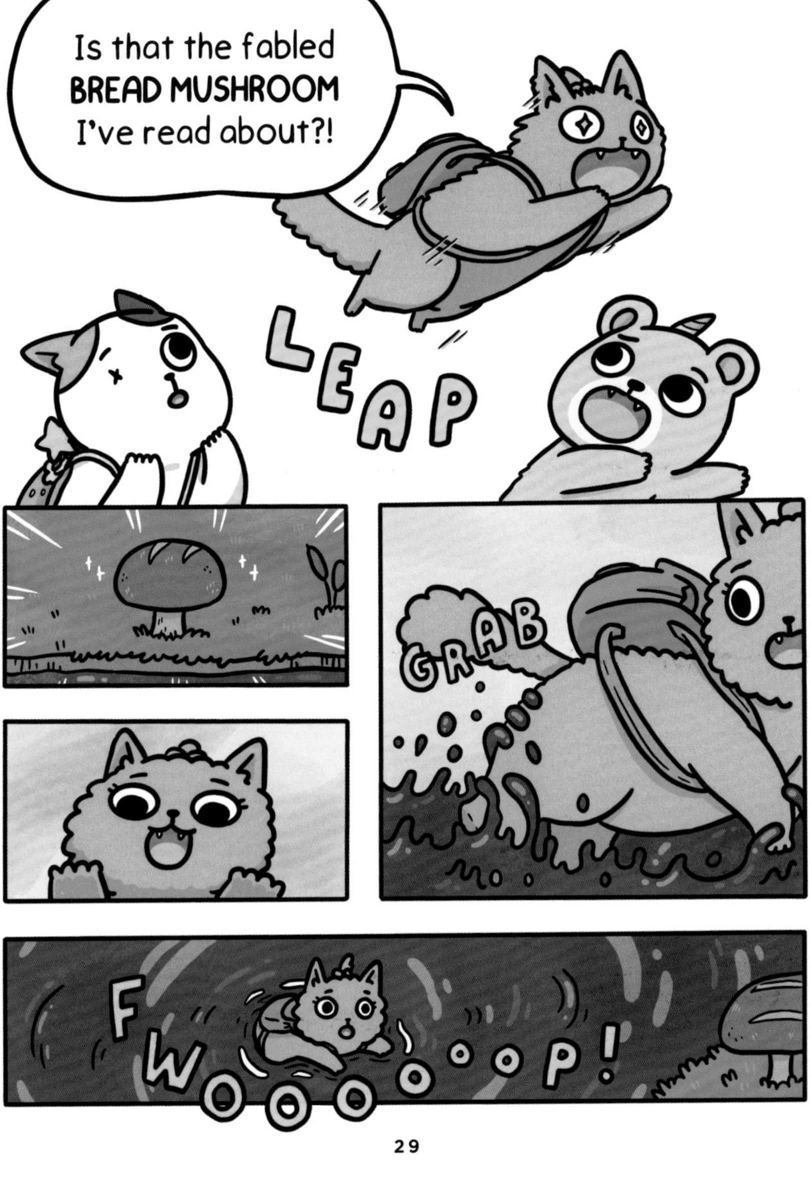
Is that the fabled BREAD MUSHROOM I've read about?!
LEAP
GRAB
FWOOOOOOP!

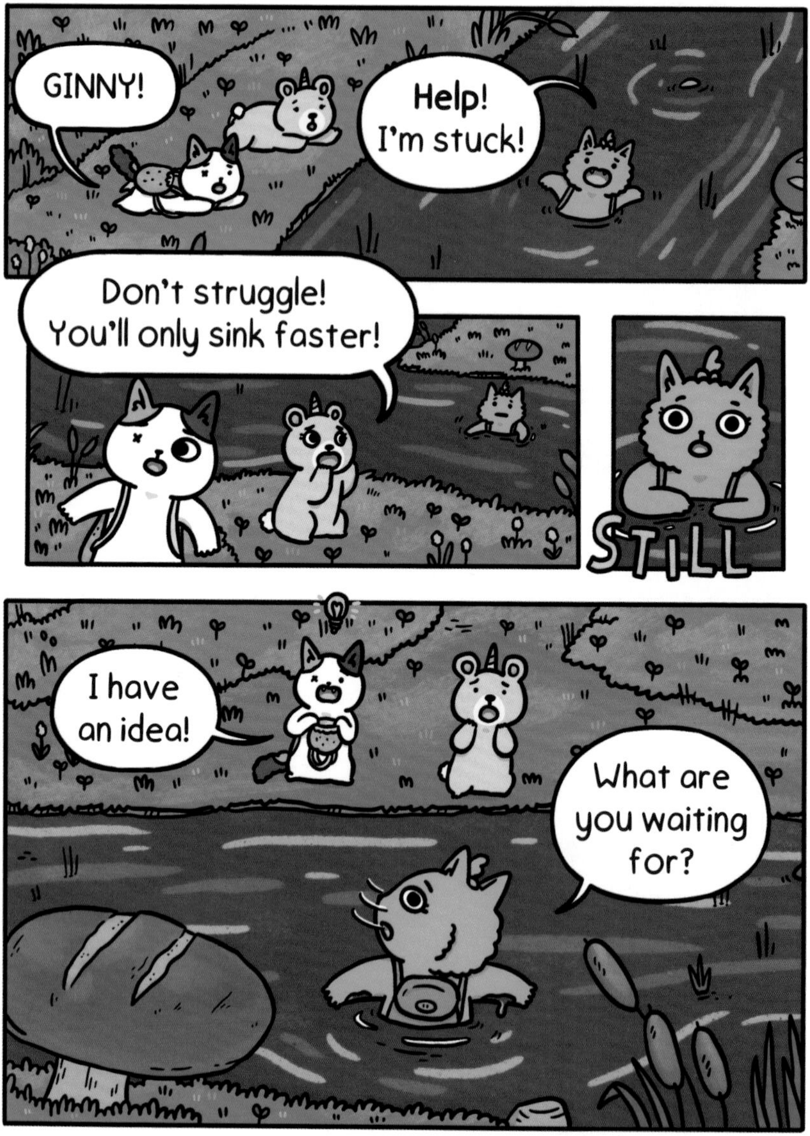
GINNY!
Help! I'm stuck!
Don't struggle! You'll only sink faster!
STILL
I have an idea!
What are you waiting for?

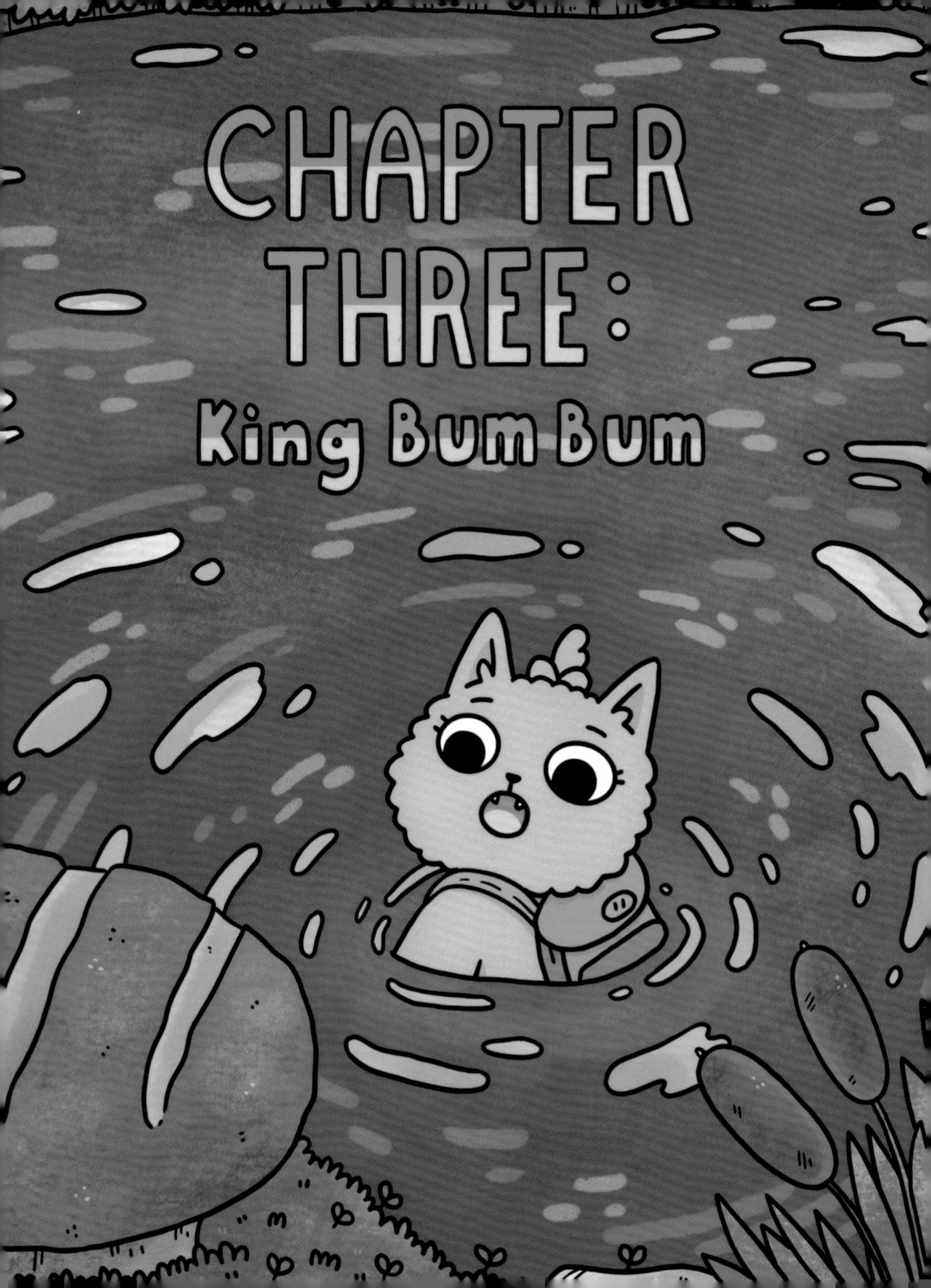
CHAPTER THREE:
King Bum Bum

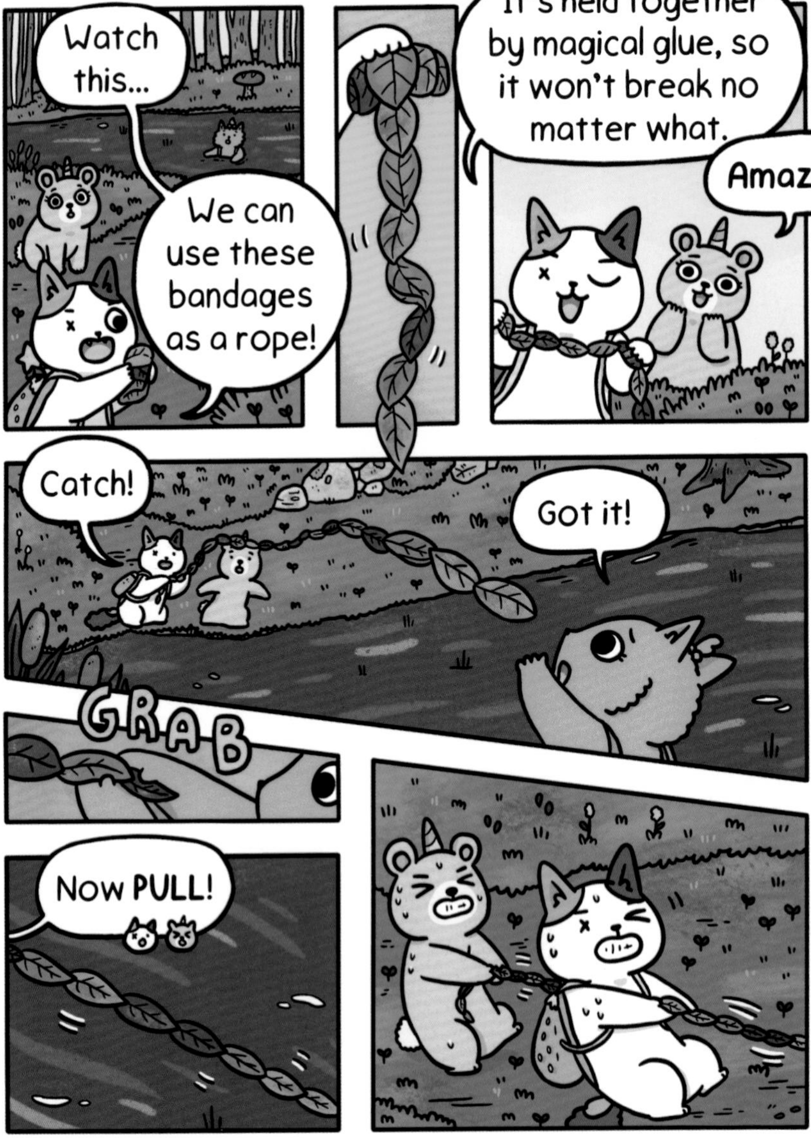
Watch this...
We can use these bandages as a rope!
It's held together by magical glue, so it won't break no matter what.
Amazing!
Catch!
Got it!
GRAB
Now PULL!

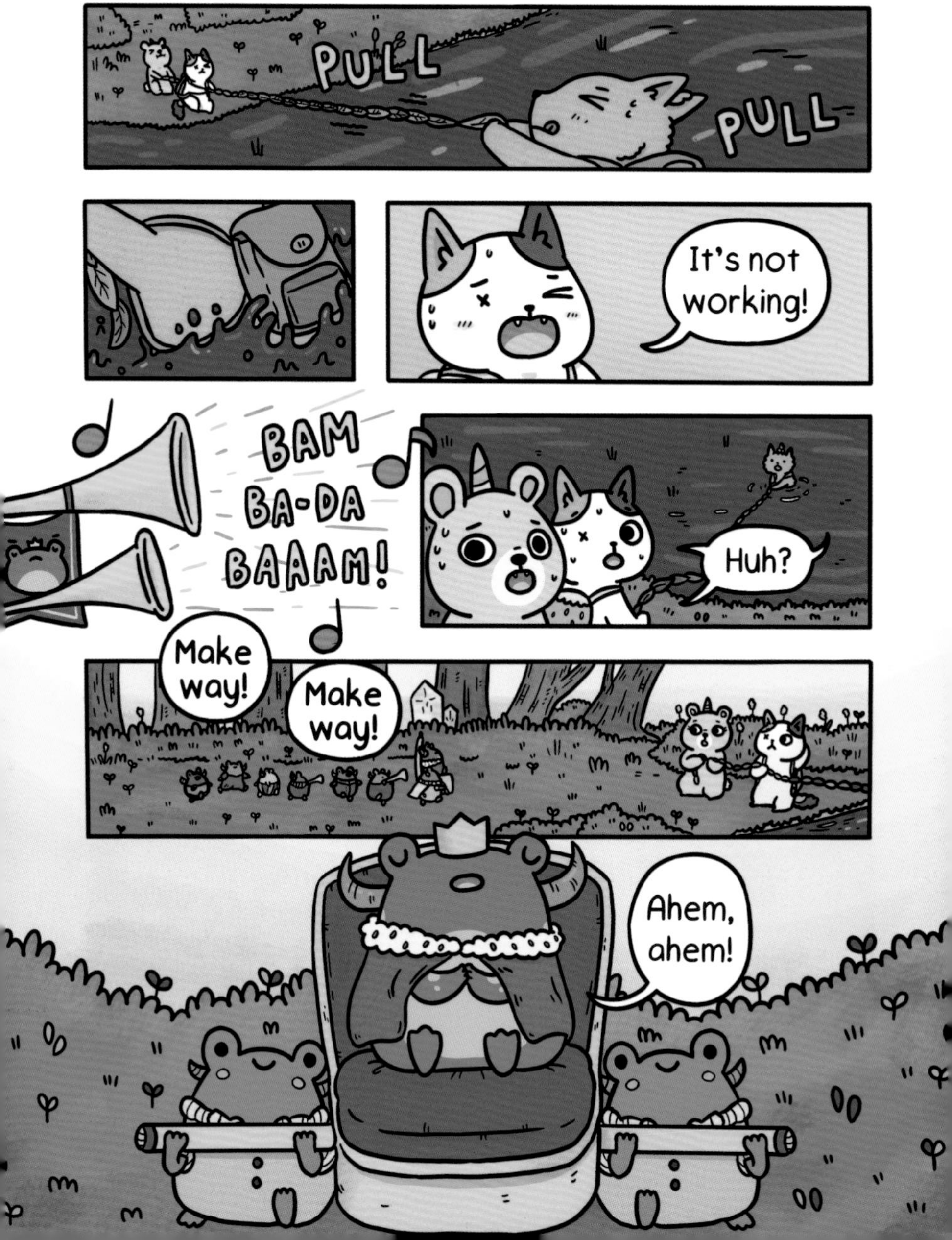
PULL
PULL
It's not working!
BAM BA-DA BAAAM!
Huh?
Make way!
Make way!
Ahem, ahem!

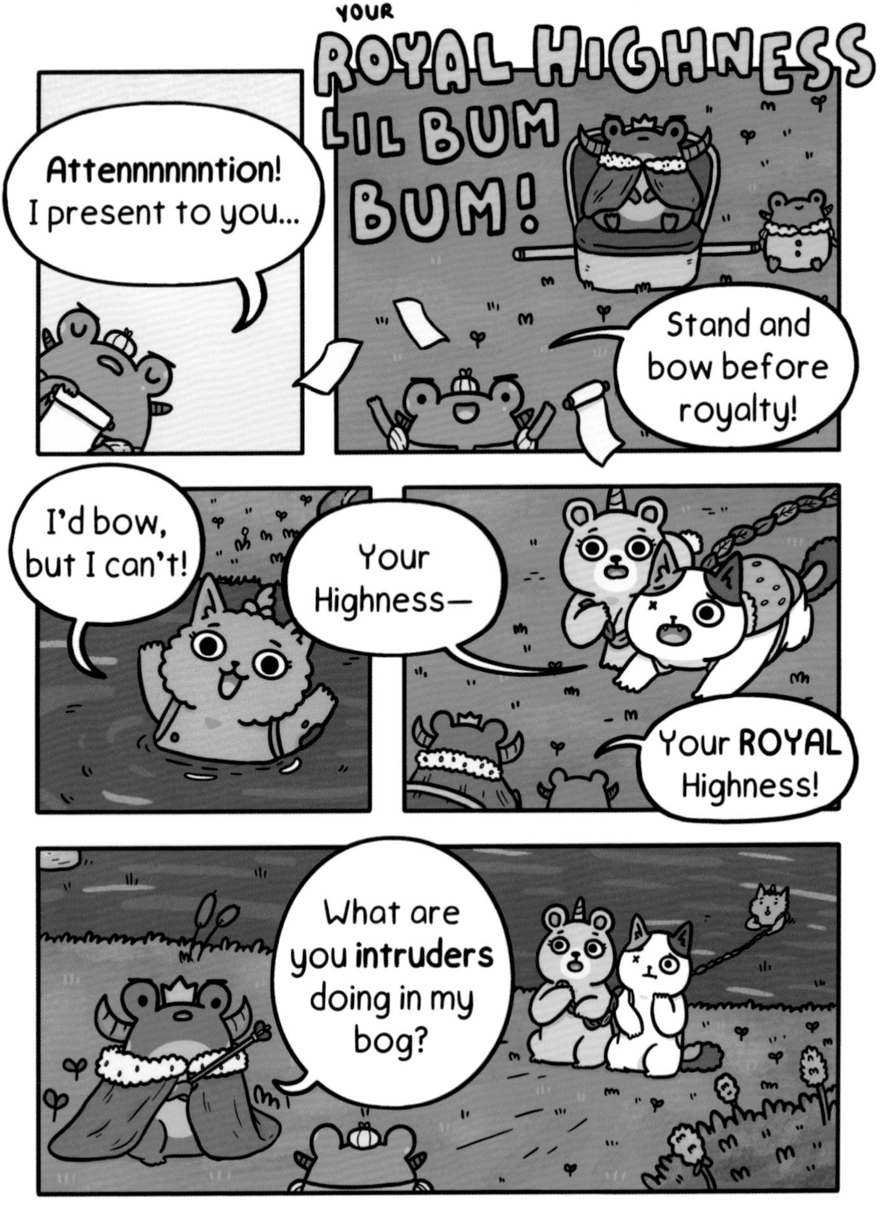
Attennnnnntion! I present to you...
YOUR ROYAL HIGHNESS LIL BUM BUM!
Stand and bow before royalty!
I'd bow, but I can't!
Your Highness—
Your ROYAL Highness!
What are you intruders doing in my bog?

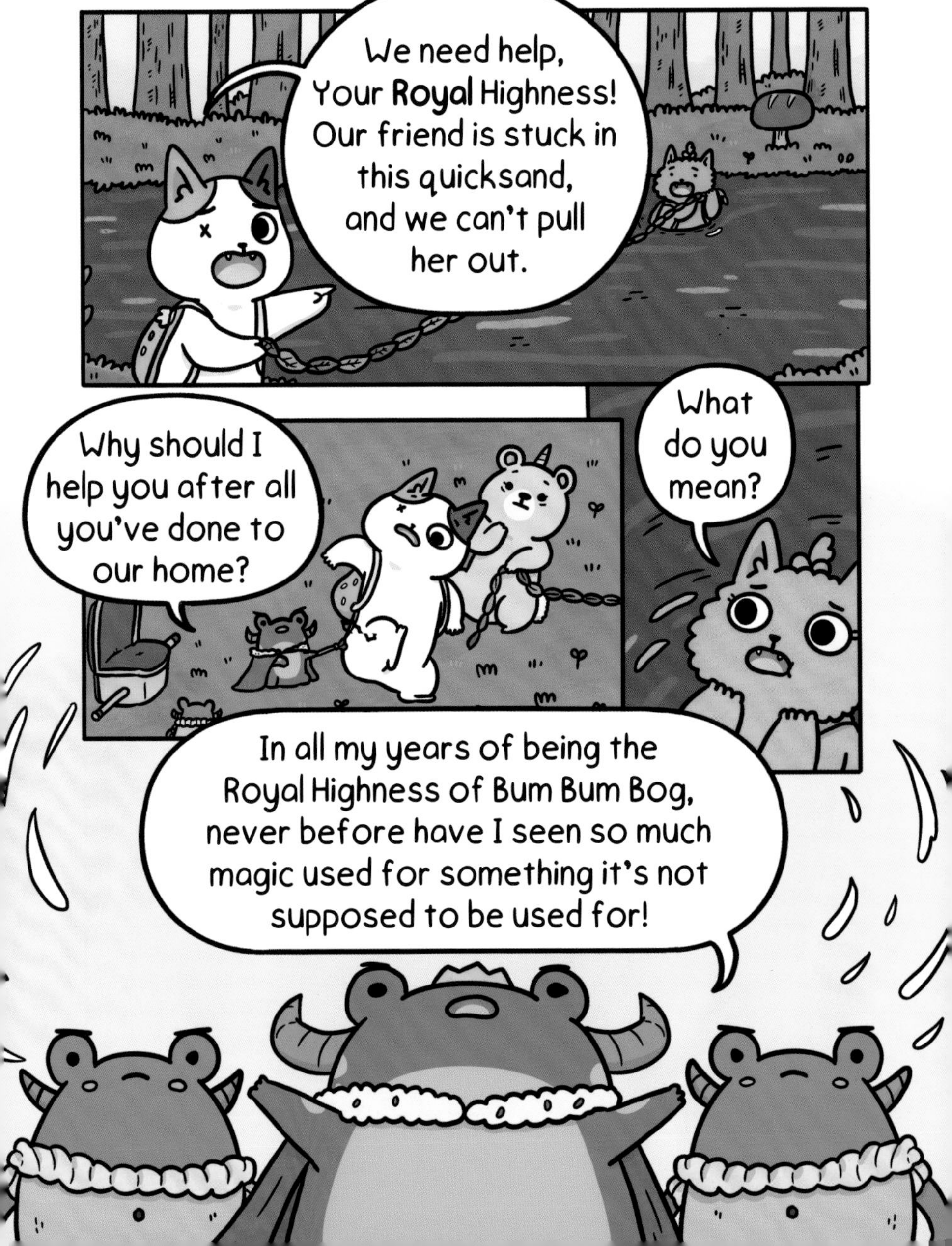
We need help, Your **Royal** Highness! Our friend is stuck in this quicksand, and we can't pull her out.
Why should I help you after all you've done to our home?
What do you mean?
In all my years of being the Royal Highness of Bum Bum Bog, never before have I seen so much magic used for something it's not supposed to be used for!

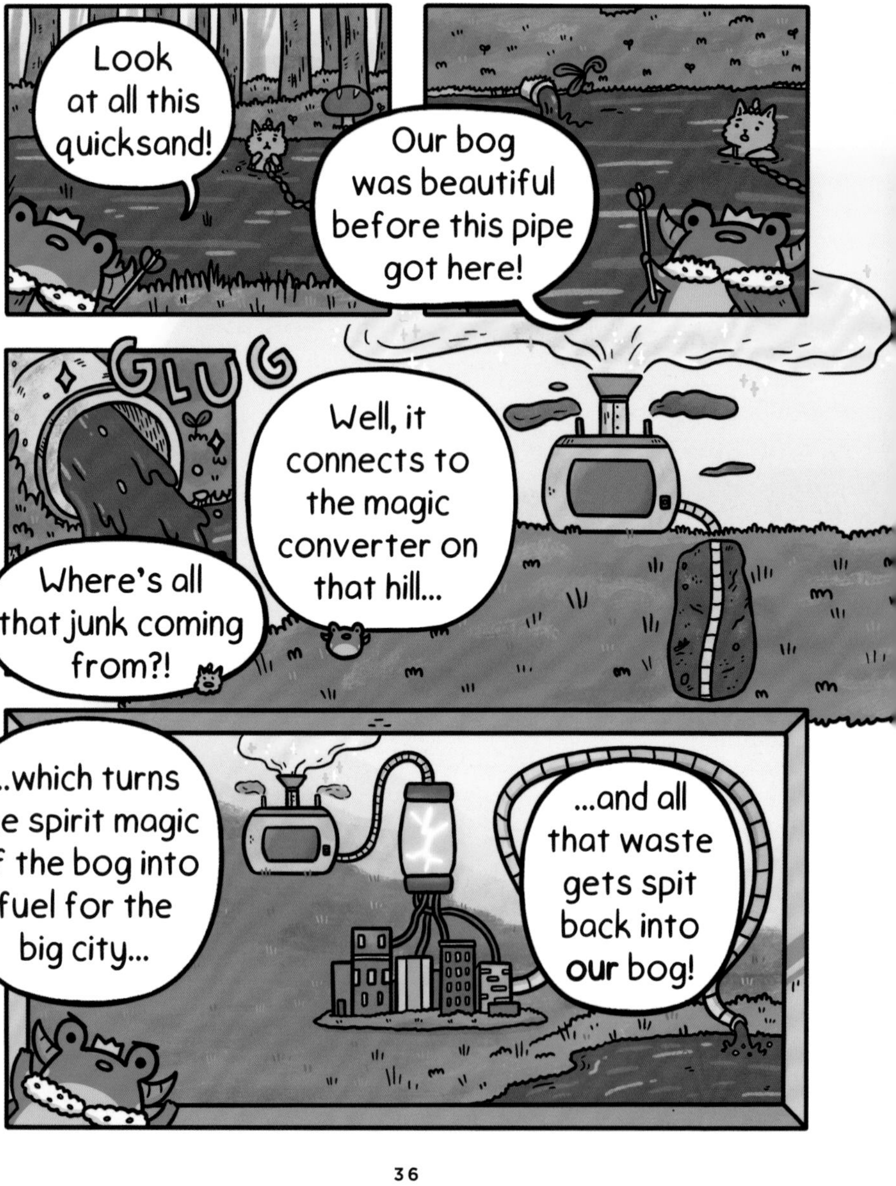
Look at all this quicksand!
Our bog was beautiful before this pipe got here!
GLUG
Where's all that junk coming from?!
Well, it connects to the magic converter on that hill...
...which turns the spirit magic of the bog into fuel for the big city...
...and all that waste gets spit back into our bog!

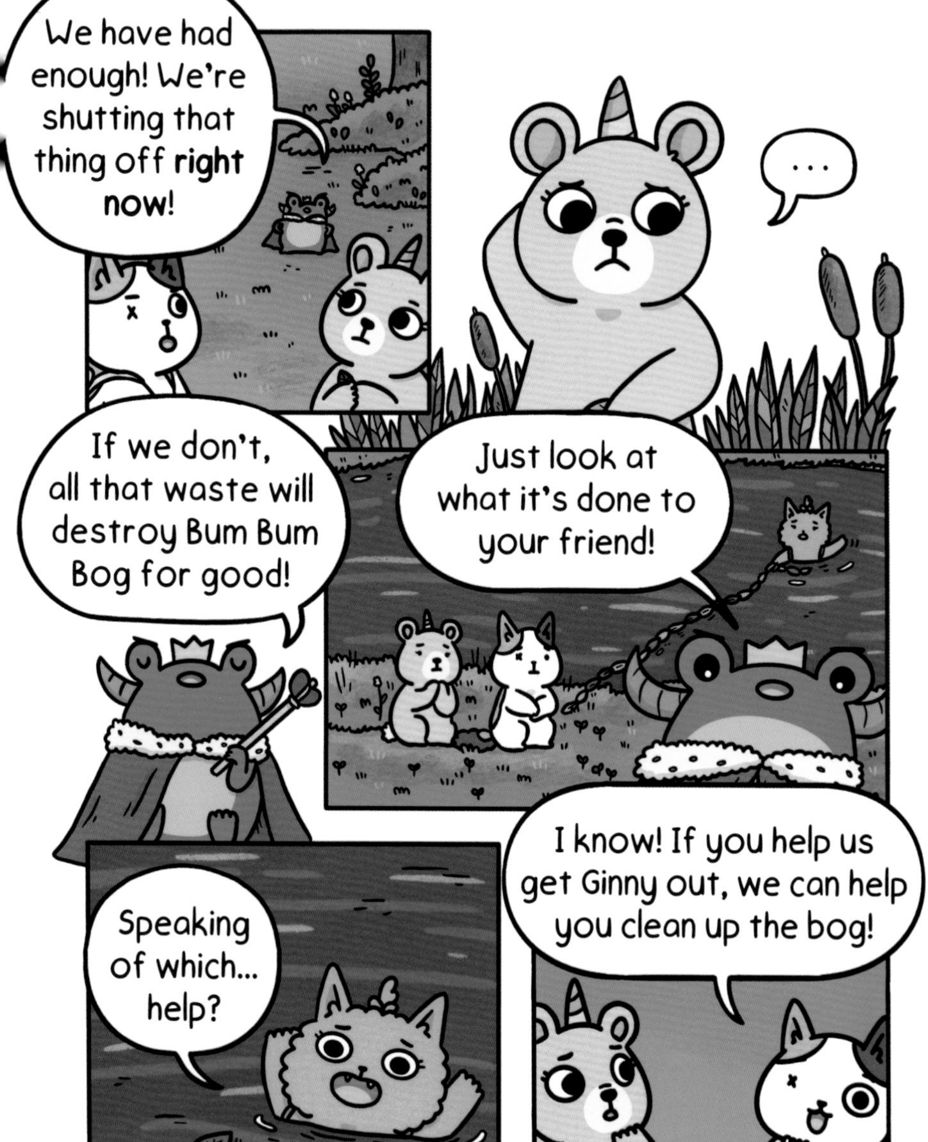
We have had enough! We're shutting that thing off **right** **now!**
...
If we don't, all that waste will destroy Bum Bum Bog for good!
Just look at what it's done to your friend!
Speaking of which... help?
I know! If you help us get Ginny out, we can help you clean up the bog!

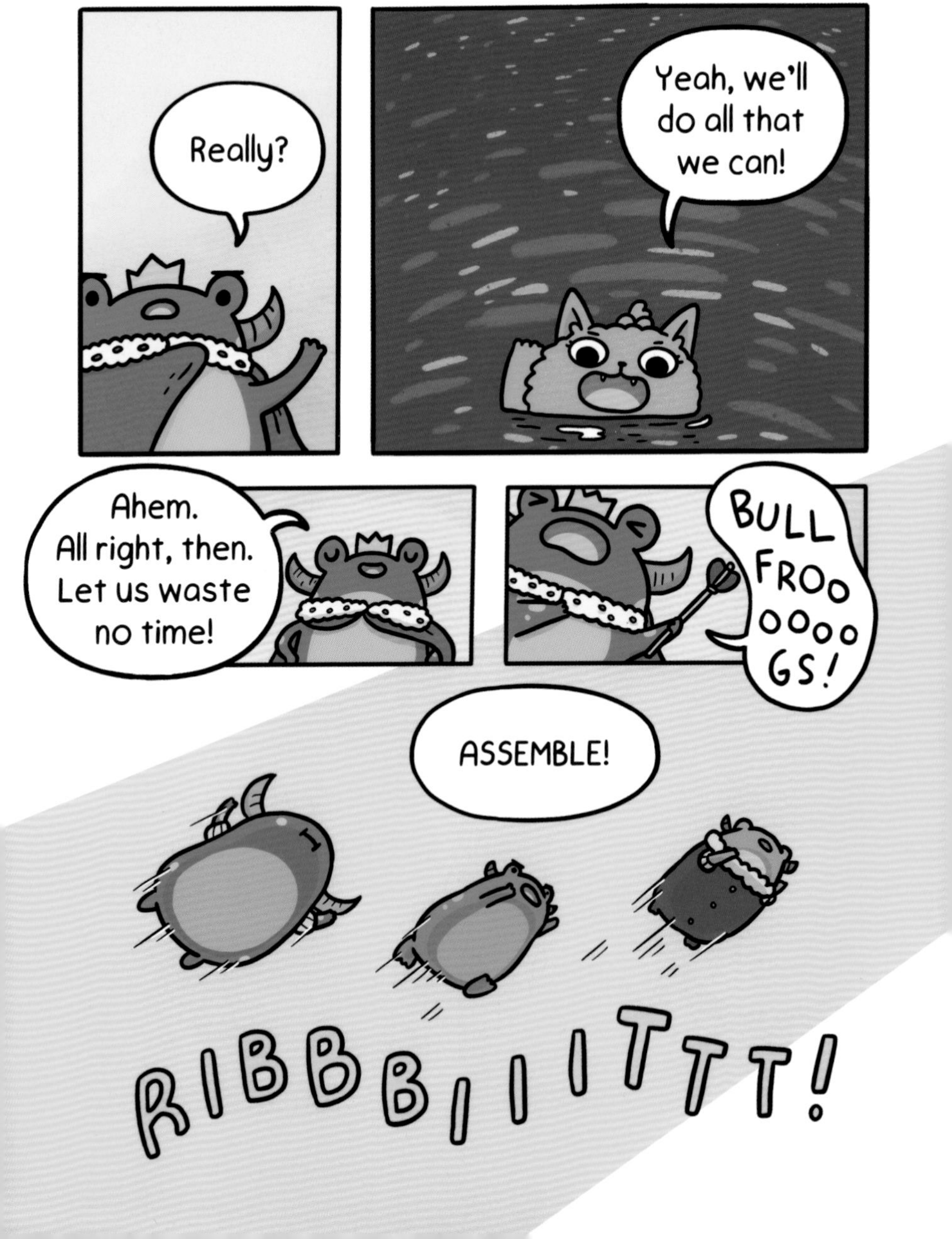
Really?
Yeah, we'll do all that we can!
Ahem. All right, then. Let us waste no time!
BULL FROOOOOOGS!
ASSEMBLE!
RIBBBIIITTT!

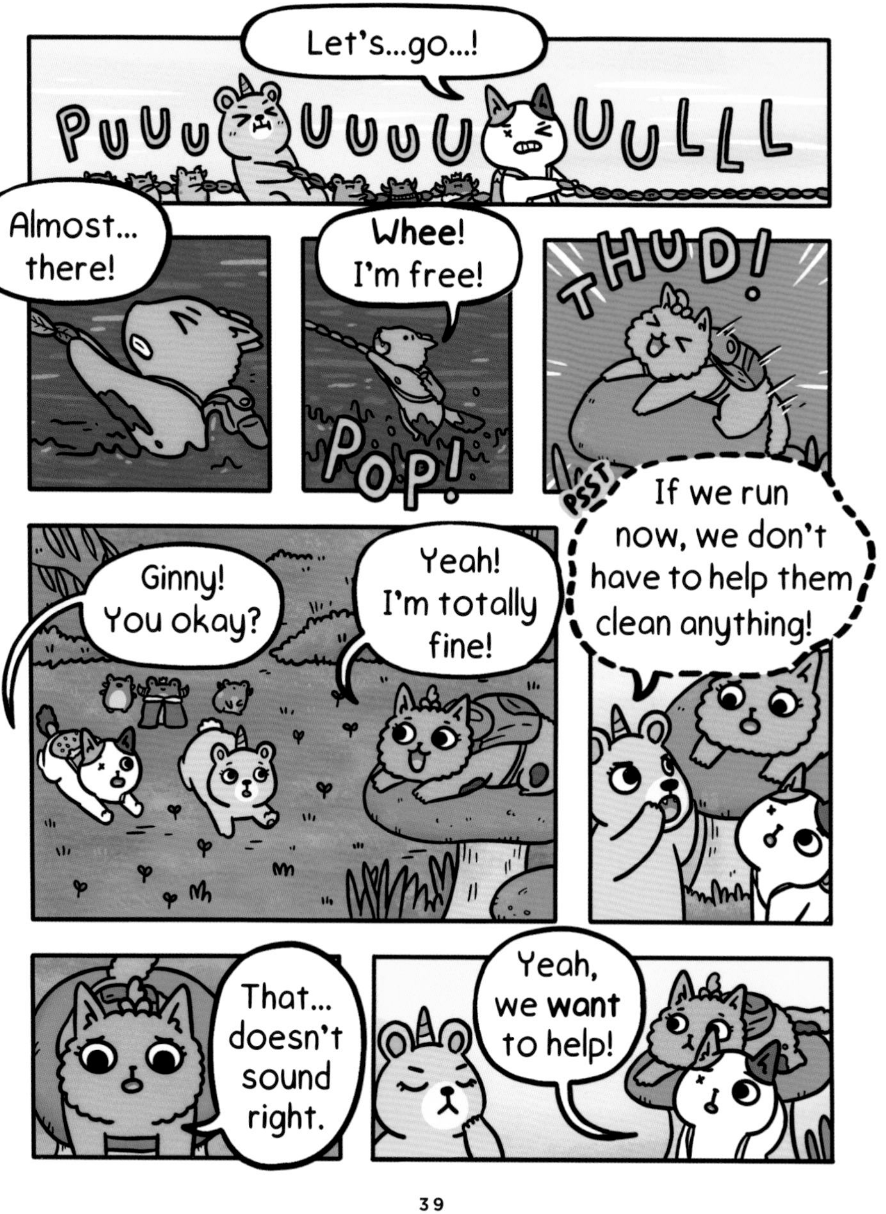
Let's...go...!
PUUUUUUUUUULLL
Almost... there!
Whee! I'm free!
POP!
THUD!
PSST
If we run now, we don't have to help them clean anything!
Ginny! You okay?
Yeah! I'm totally fine!
That... doesn't sound right.
Yeah, we **want** to help!

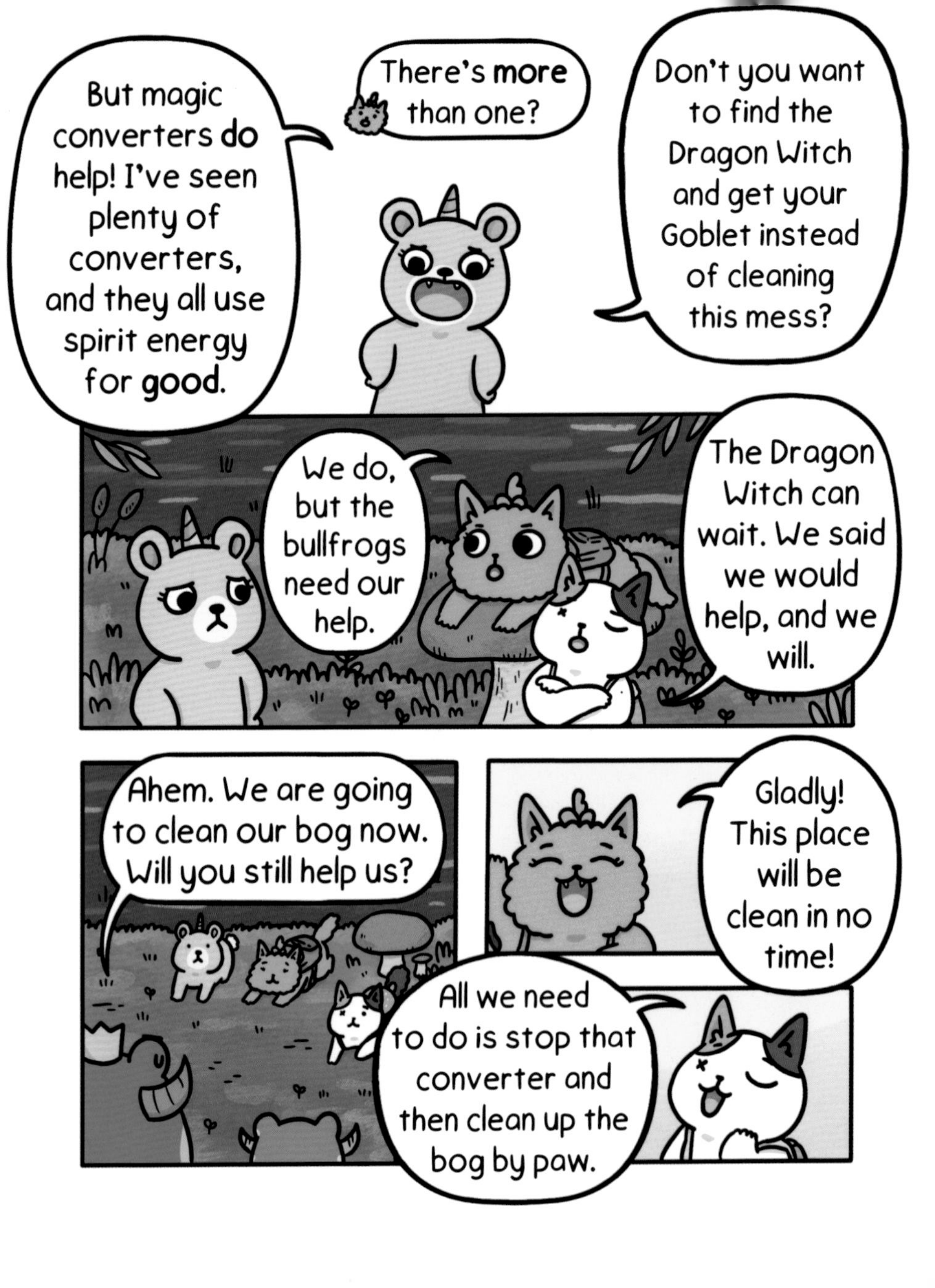

But magic converters do help! I've seen plenty of converters, and they all use spirit energy for good.
There's more than one?
Don't you want to find the Dragon Witch and get your Goblet instead of cleaning this mess?
We do, but the bullfrogs need our help.
The Dragon Witch can wait. We said we would help, and we will.
Ahem. We are going to clean our bog now. Will you still help us?
Gladly! This place will be clean in no time!
All we need to do is stop that converter and then clean up the bog by paw.

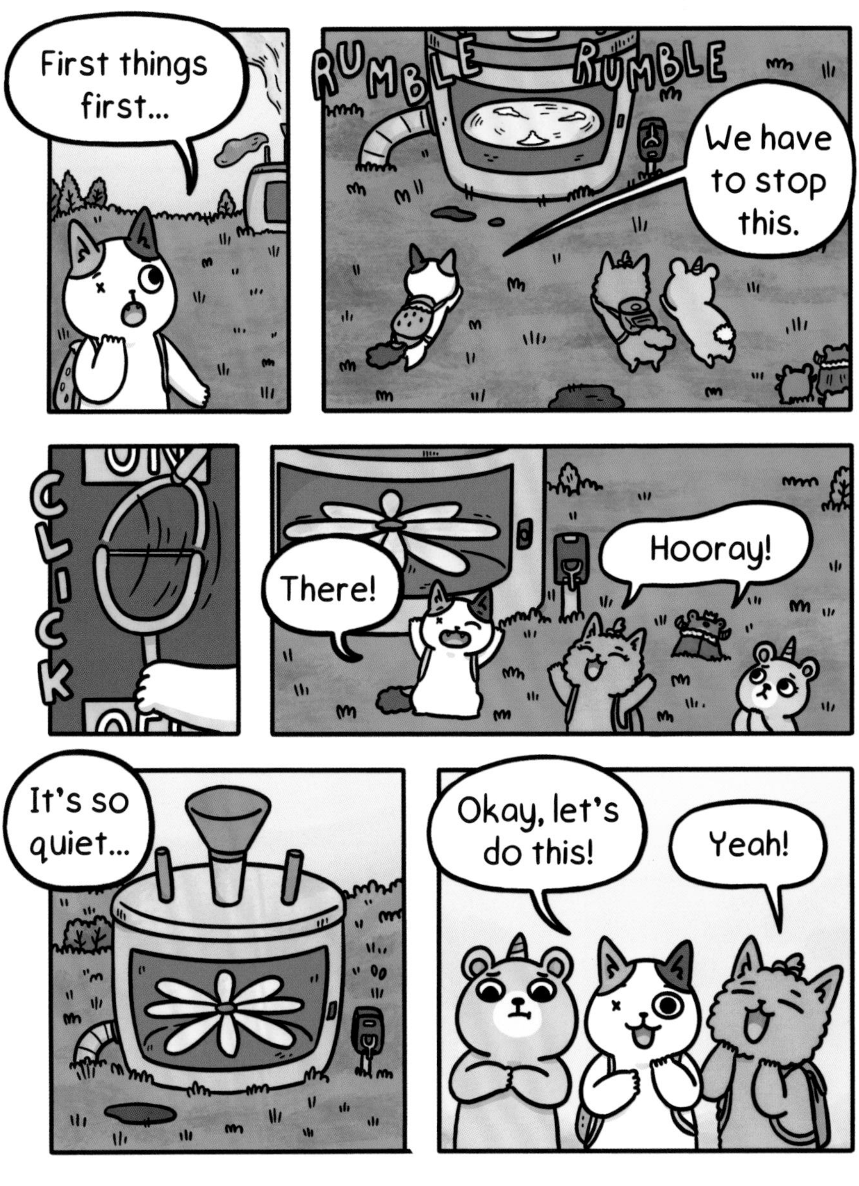
First things first...
RUMBLE RUMBLE
We have to stop this.
CLICK
There!
Hooray!
It's so quiet...
Okay, let's do this!
Yeah!

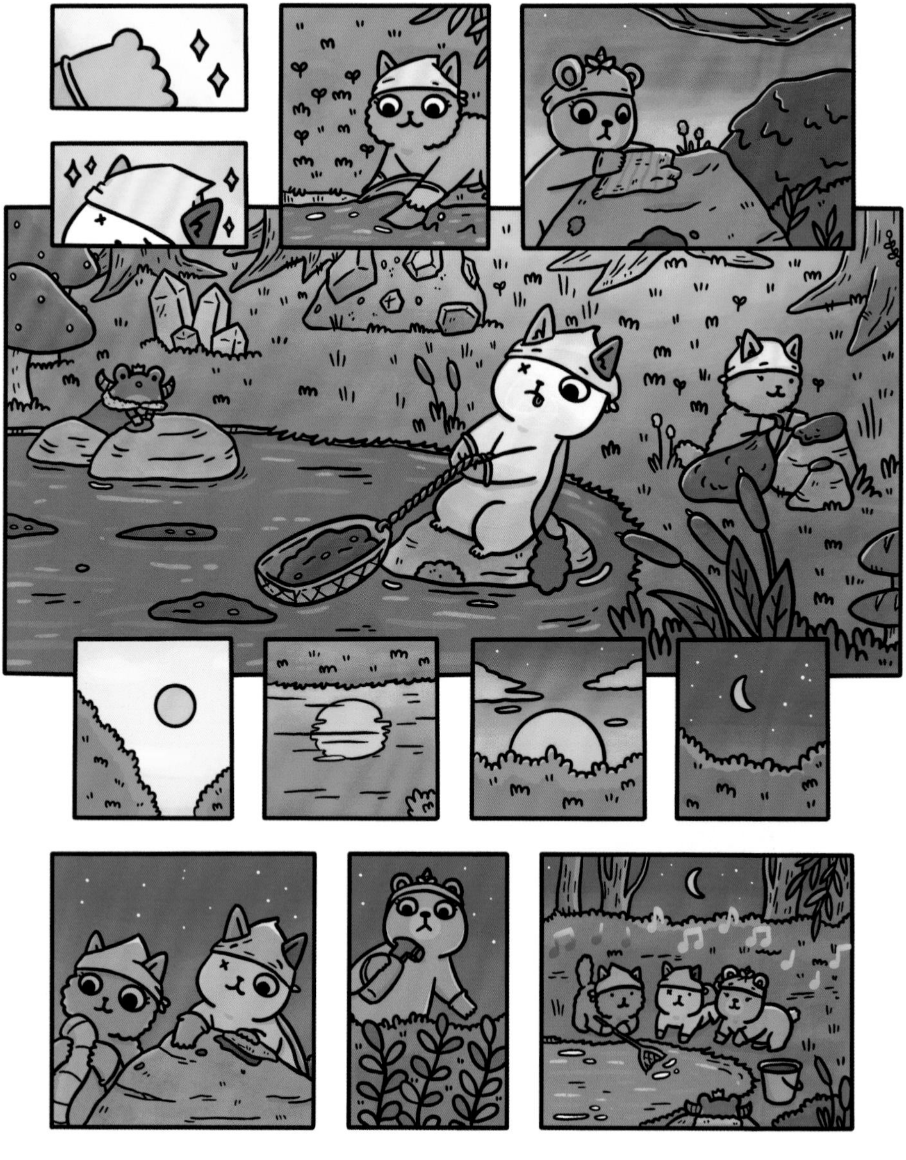

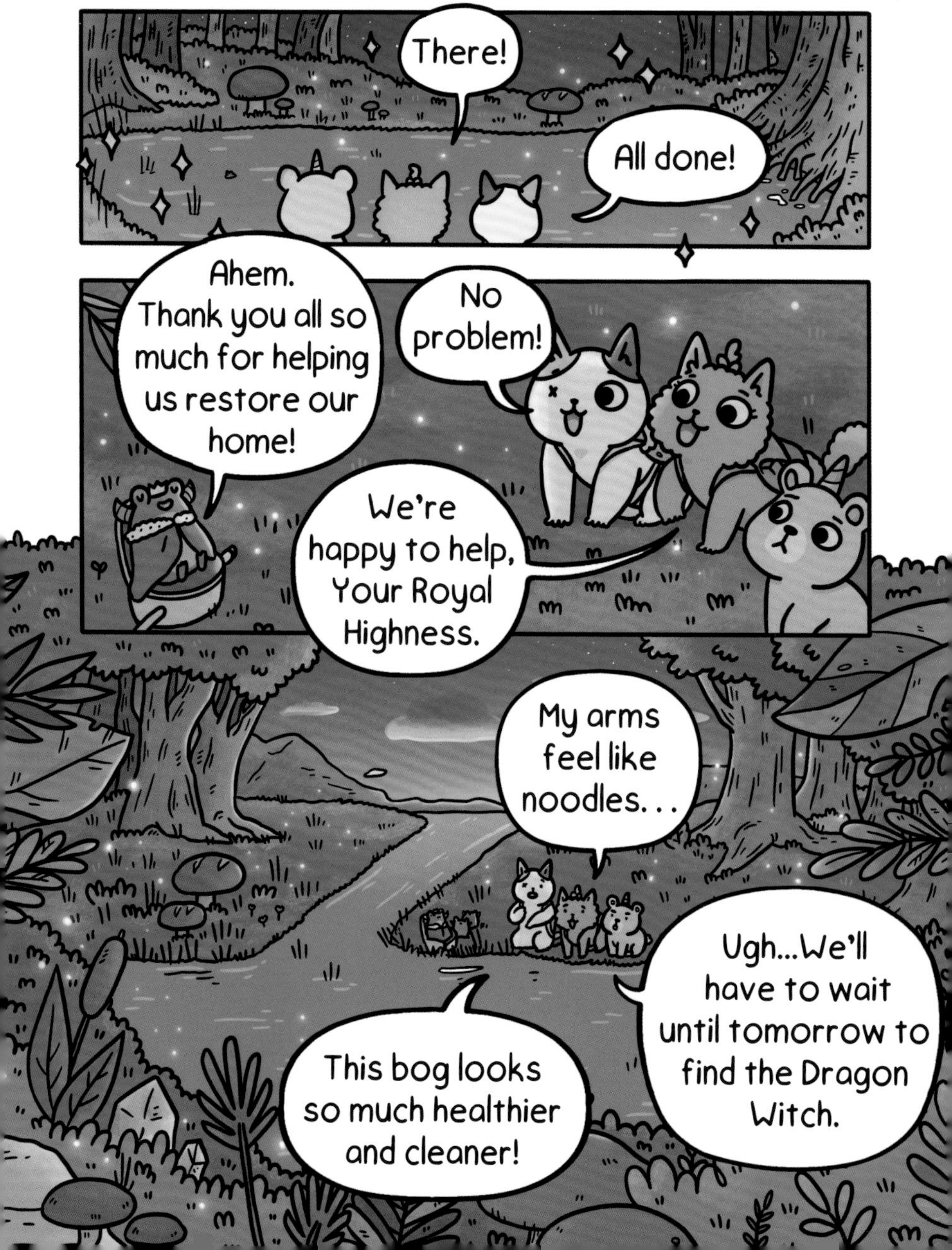
There!
All done!
Ahem. Thank you all so much for helping us restore our home!
No problem!
We're happy to help, Your Royal Highness.
My arms feel like noodles. . .
Ugh...We'll have to wait until tomorrow to find the Dragon Witch.
This bog looks so much healthier and cleaner!

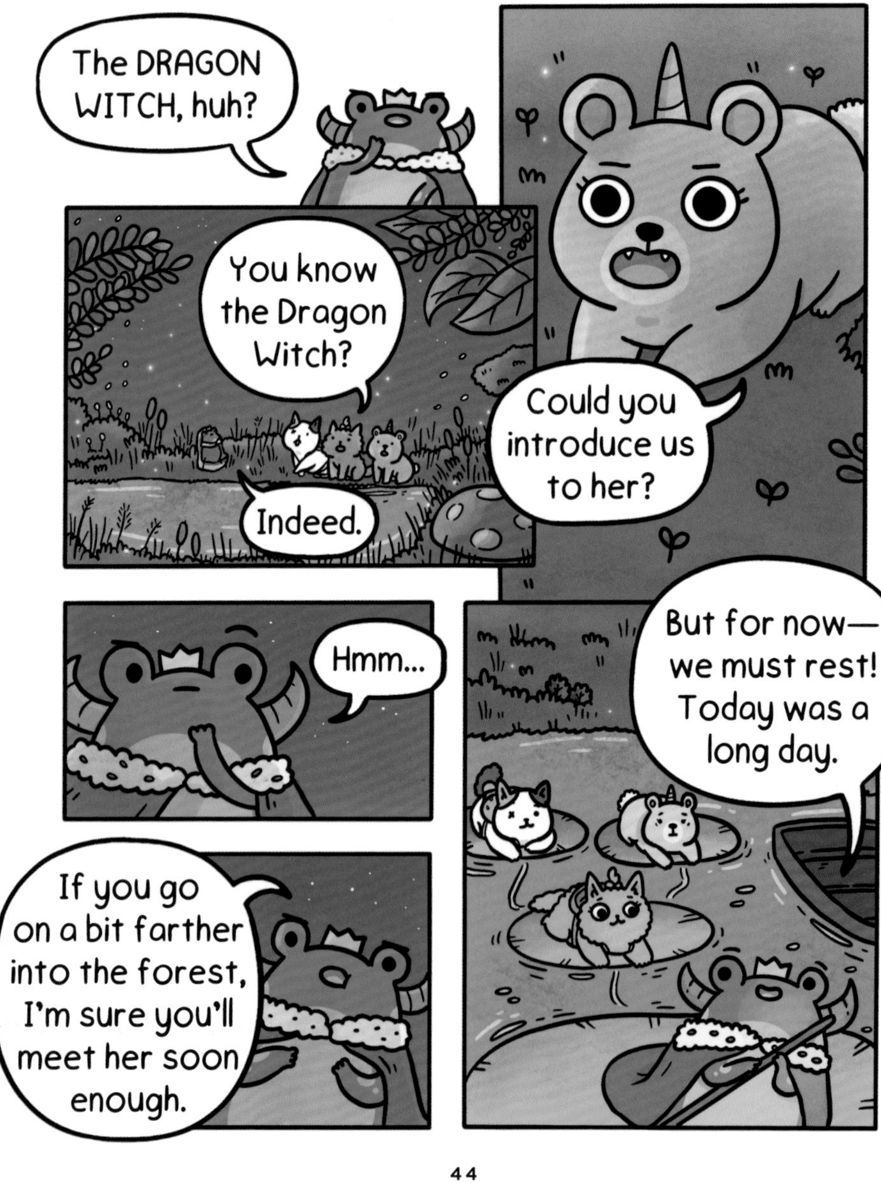
The DRAGON WITCH, huh?
You know the Dragon Witch?
Indeed.
Could you introduce us to her?
Hmm...
If you go on a bit farther into the forest, I'm sure you'll meet her soon enough.
But for now— we must rest! Today was a long day.

Moments later...

These are our newly renovated chambers.

You may stay here for tonight.

Thank you!

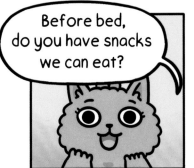

Before bed, do you have snacks we can eat?

Of course! Come join us for dinner whenever you are ready!

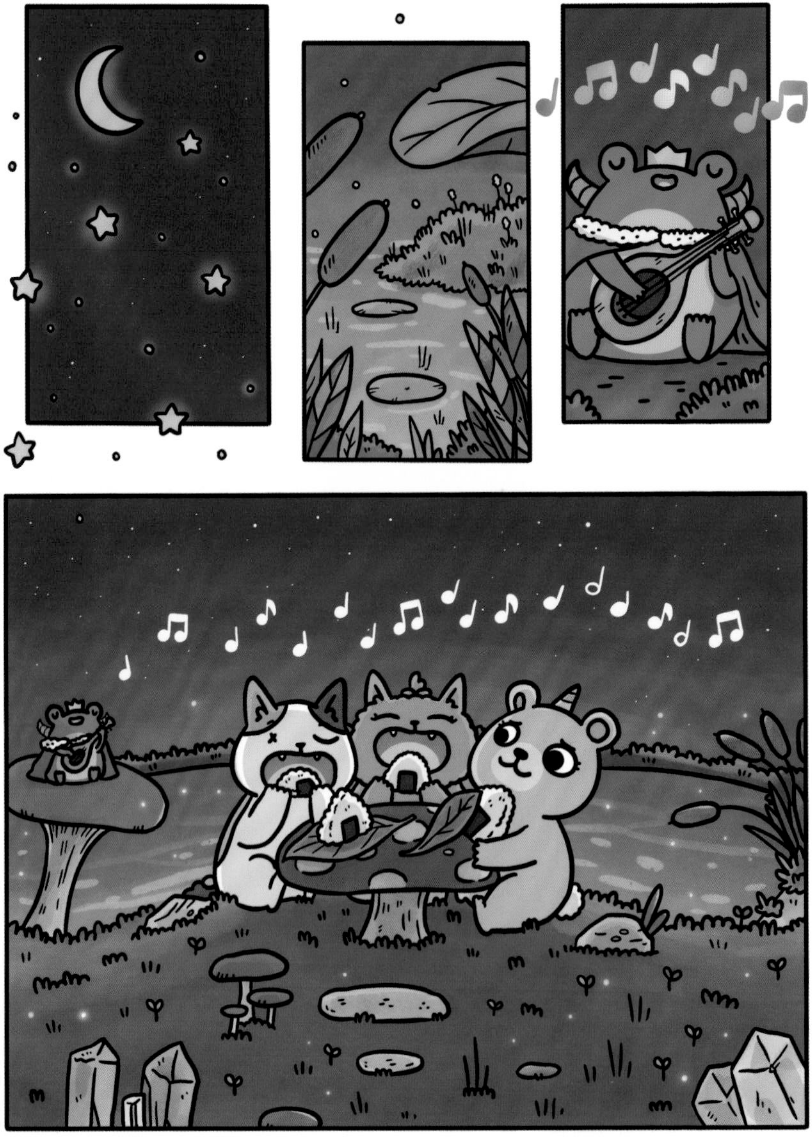

CHAPTER FOUR: Cinder

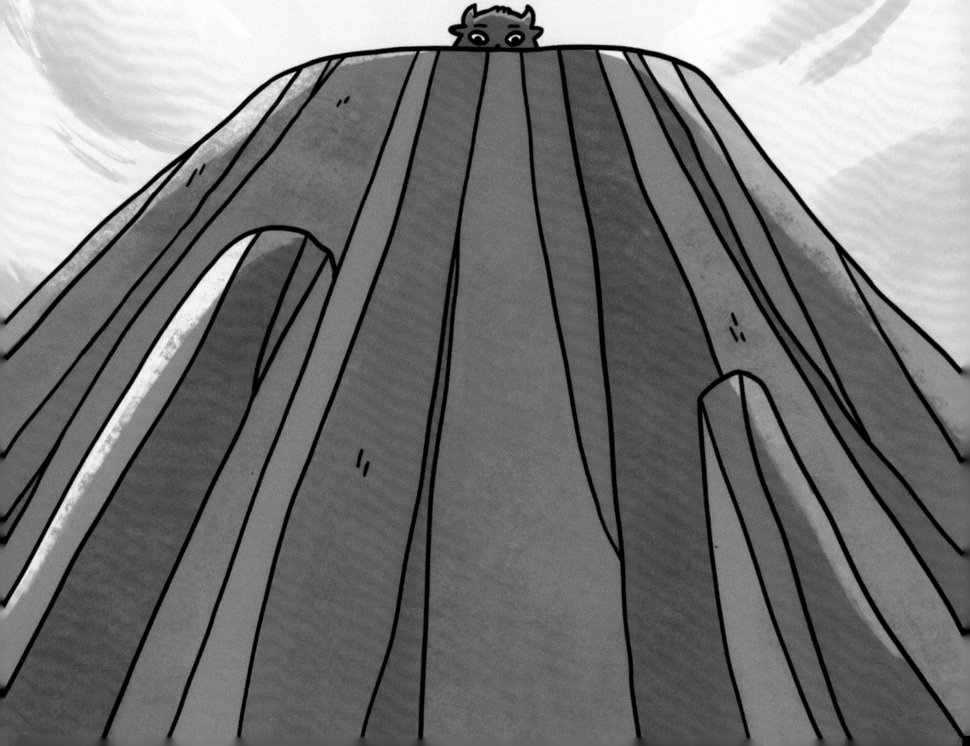

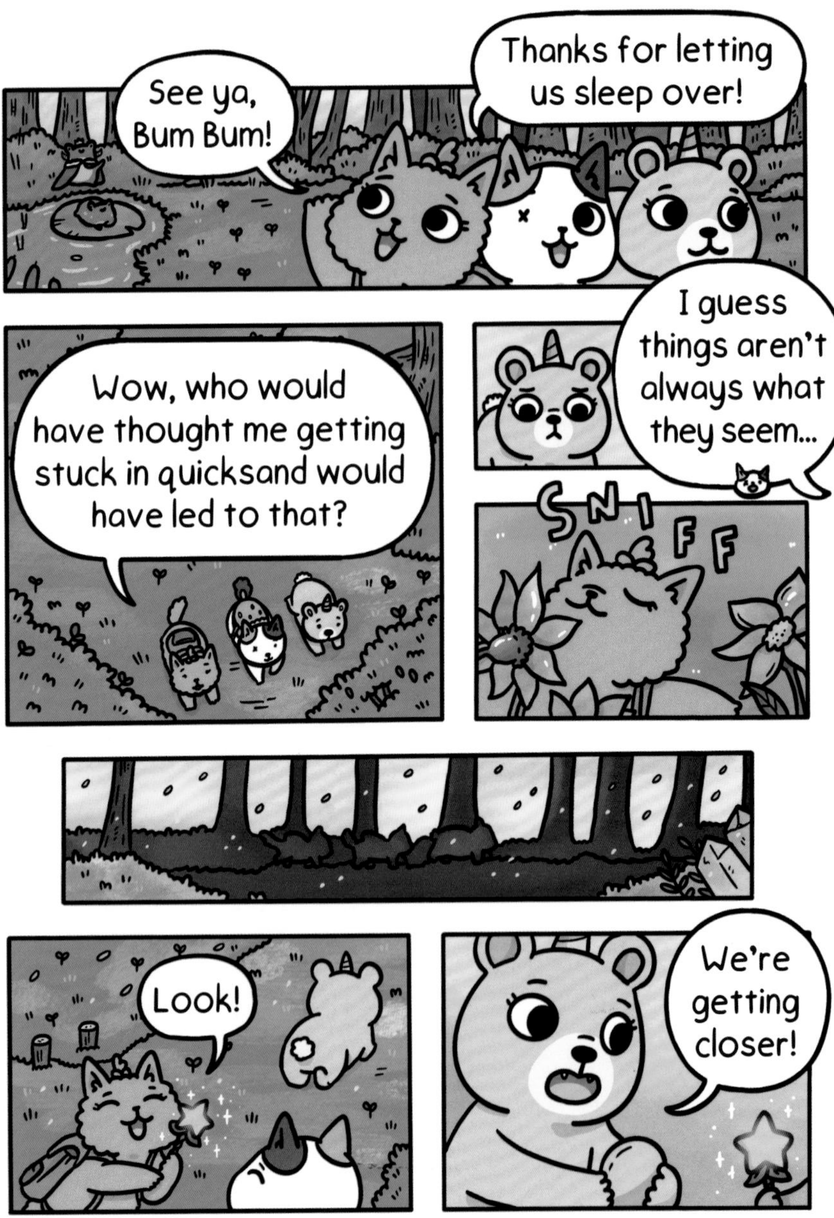
See ya, Bum Bum!
Thanks for letting us sleep over!
Wow, who would have thought me getting stuck in quicksand would have led to that?
I guess things aren't always what they seem...
SNIFF
Look!
We're getting closer!

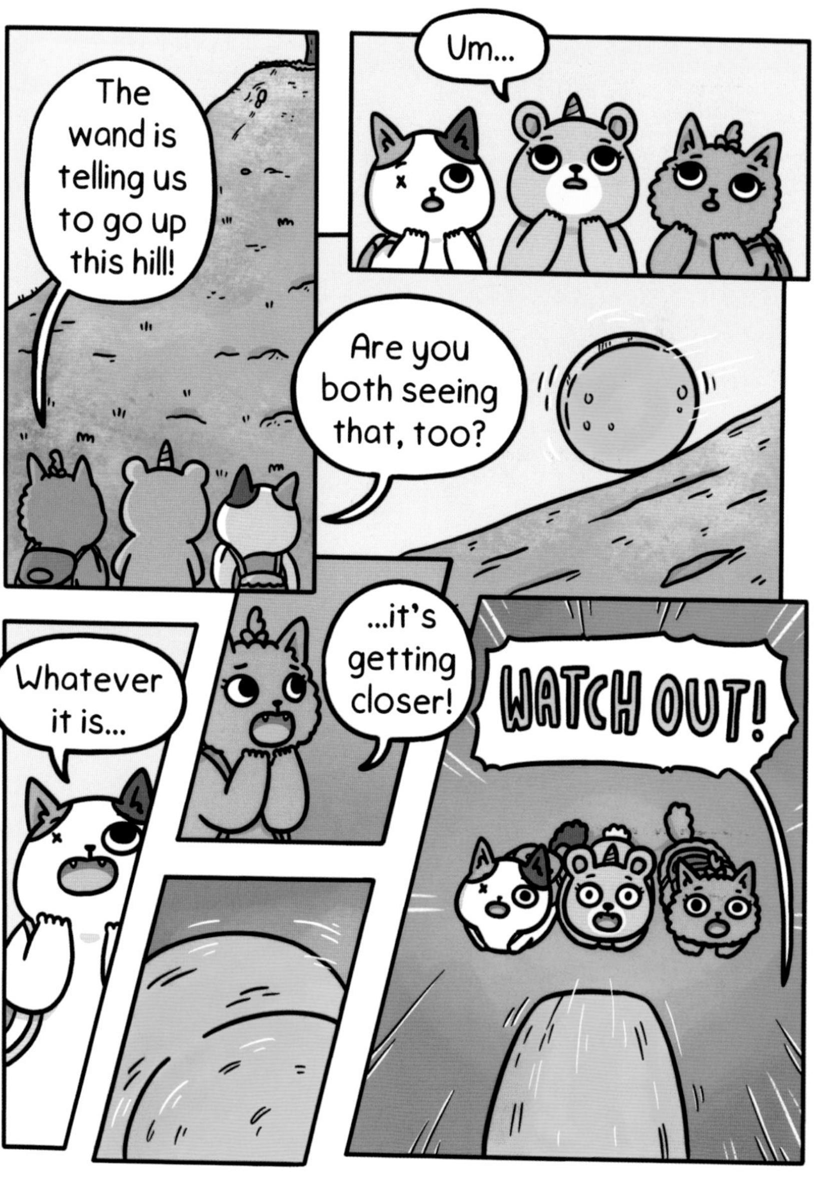
The wand is telling us to go up this hill!
Um...
Are you both seeing that, too?
Whatever it is...
...it's getting closer!
WATCH OUT!

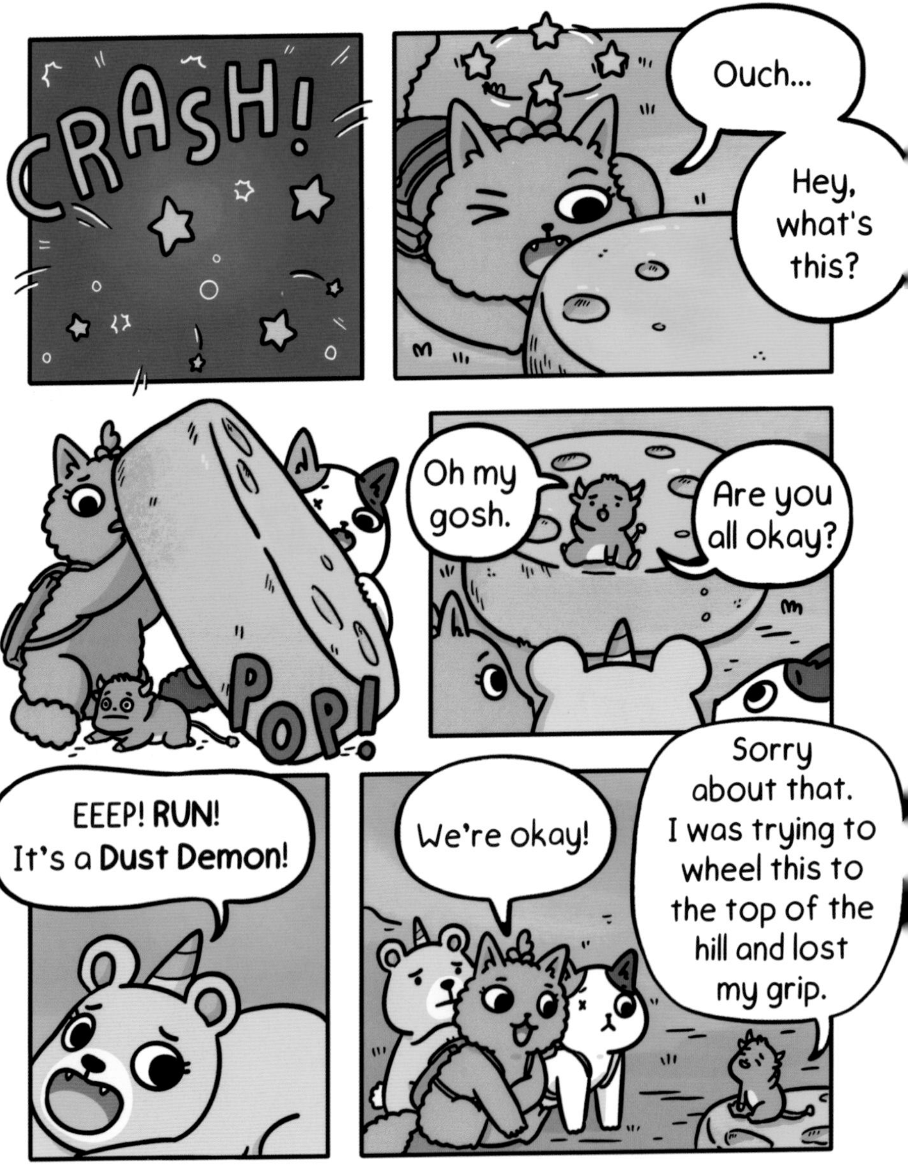
CRASH!
Ouch...
Hey, what's this?
POP!
Oh my gosh.
Are you all okay?
EEEP! **RUN!** It's a **Dust Demon!**
We're okay!
Sorry about that. I was trying to wheel this to the top of the hill and lost my grip.

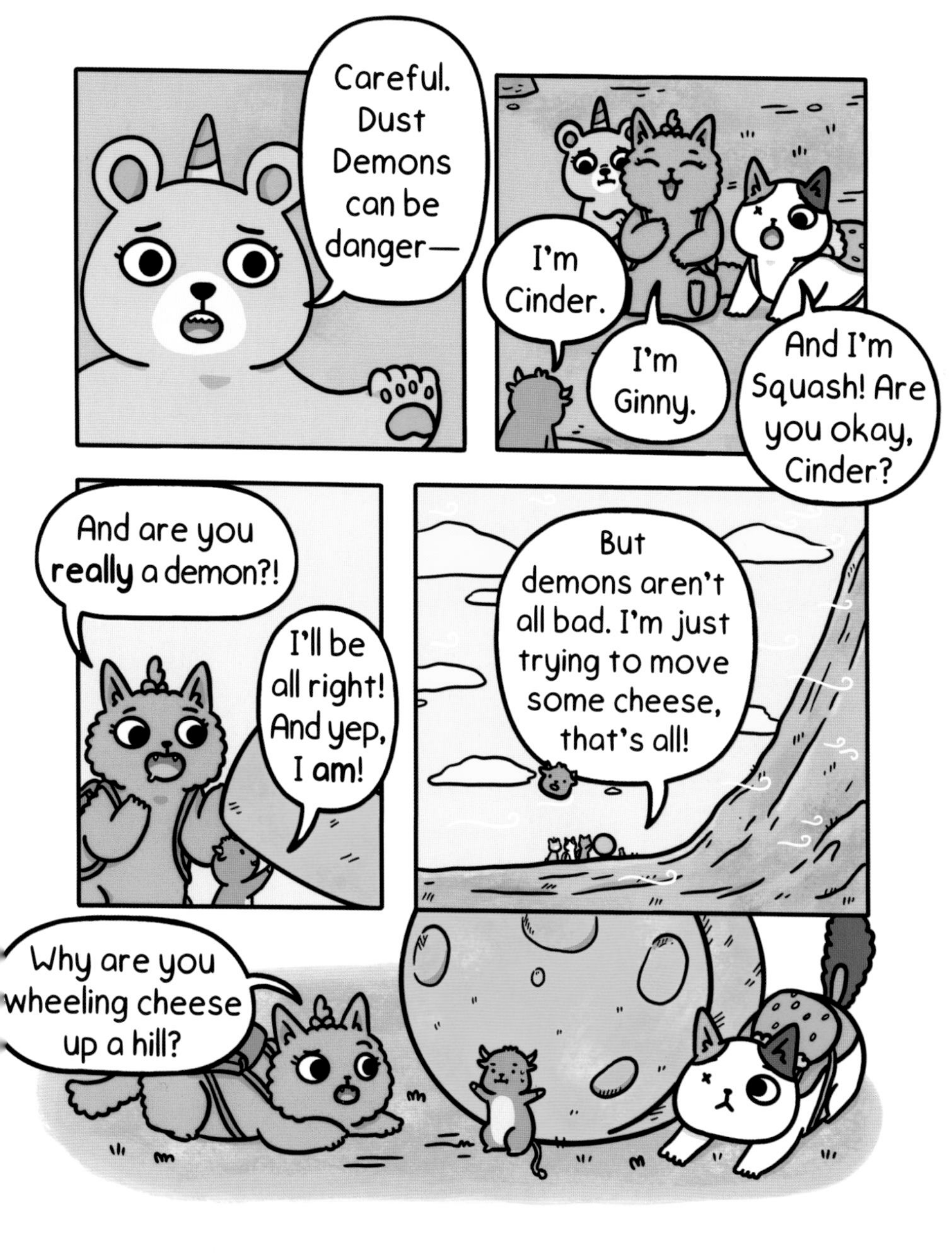
Careful. Dust Demons can be danger—
I'm Cinder.
I'm Ginny.
And I'm Squash! Are you okay, Cinder?
And are you **really** a demon?!
I'll be all right! And yep, I **am**!
But demons aren't all bad. I'm just trying to move some cheese, that's all!
Why are you wheeling cheese up a hill?

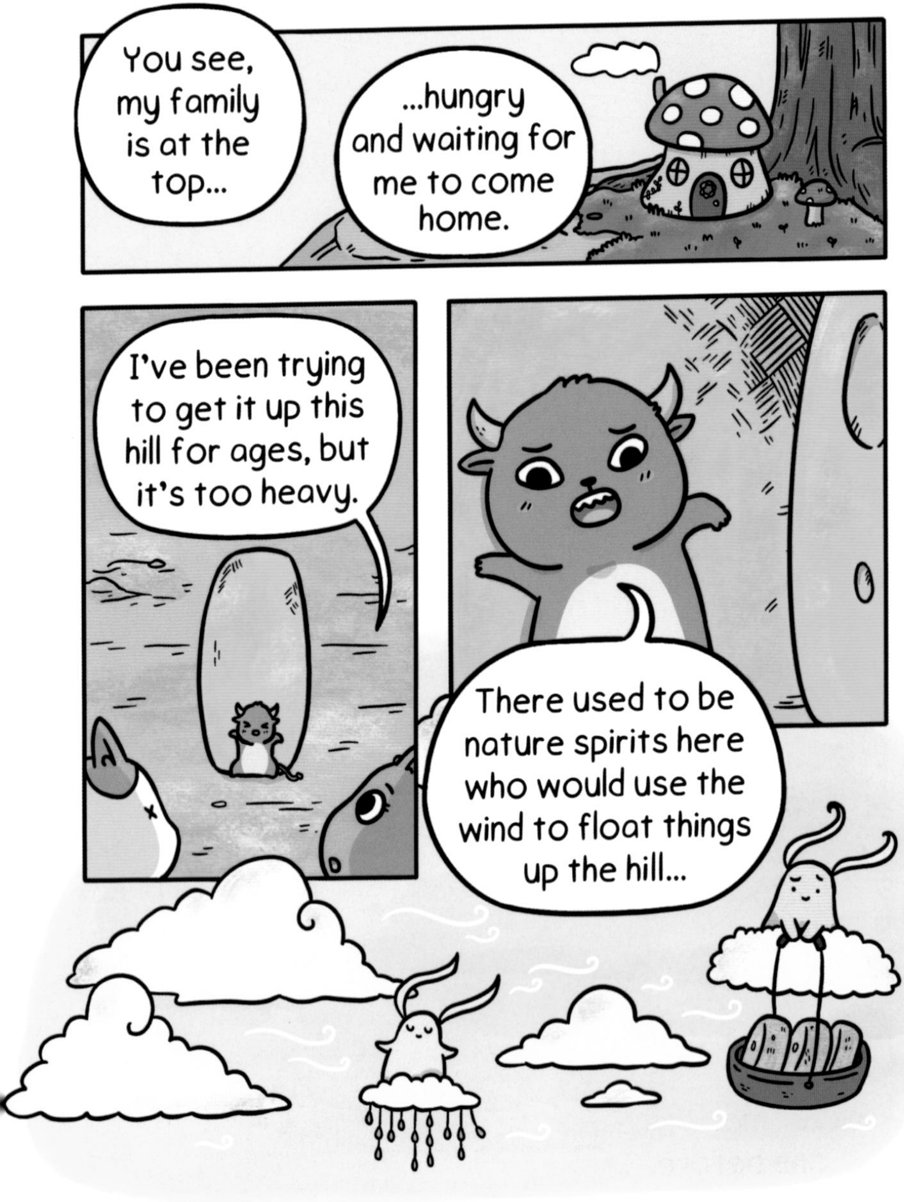
You see, my family is at the top...
...hungry and waiting for me to come home.
I've been trying to get it up this hill for ages, but it's too heavy.
There used to be nature spirits here who would use the wind to float things up the hill...

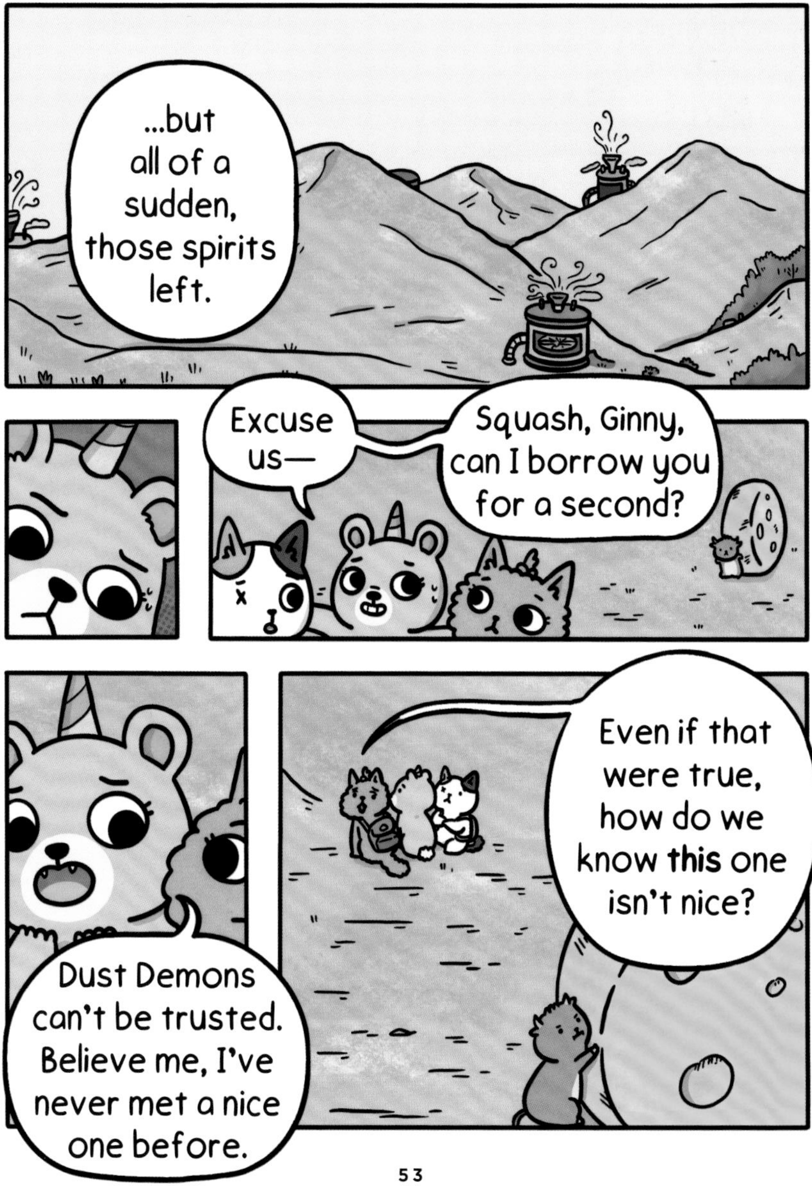
...but all of a sudden, those spirits left.
Excuse us—
Squash, Ginny, can I borrow you for a second?
Dust Demons can't be trusted. Believe me, I've never met a nice one before.
Even if that were true, how do we know **this** one isn't nice?

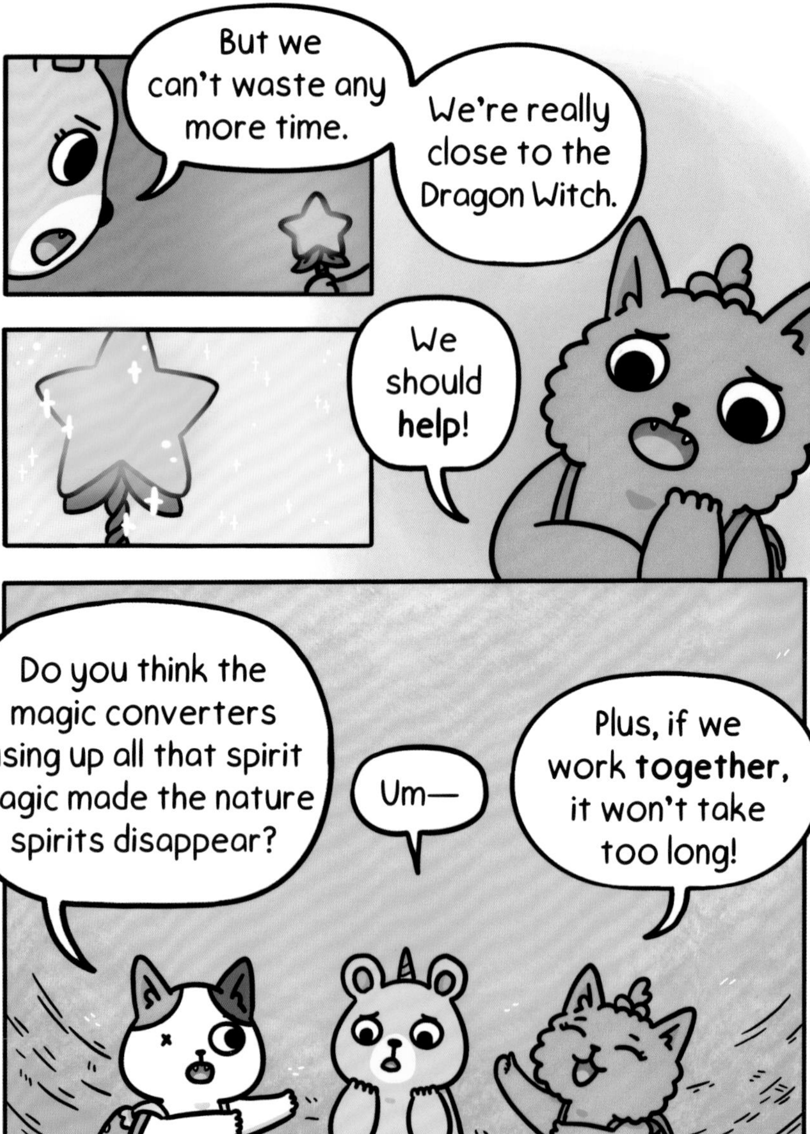

But we can't waste any more time.
We're really close to the Dragon Witch.
We should **help**!
Do you think the magic converters using up all that spirit magic made the nature spirits disappear?
Um—
Plus, if we work **together**, it won't take too long!

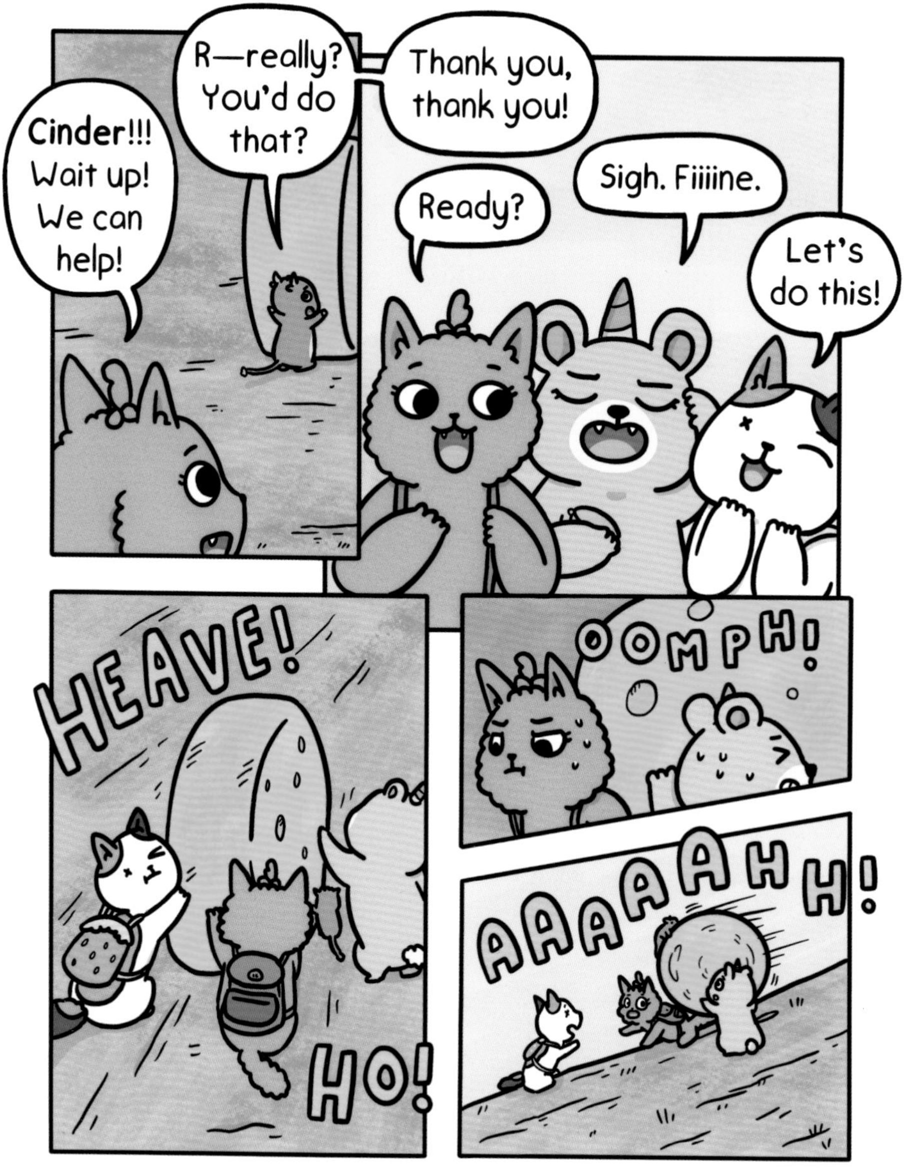

Cinder!!! Wait up! We can help!
R—really? You'd do that?
Thank you, thank you!
Ready?
Sigh. Fiiiine.
Let's do this!
HEAVE!
HO!
OOMPH!
AAAAAAHHH!

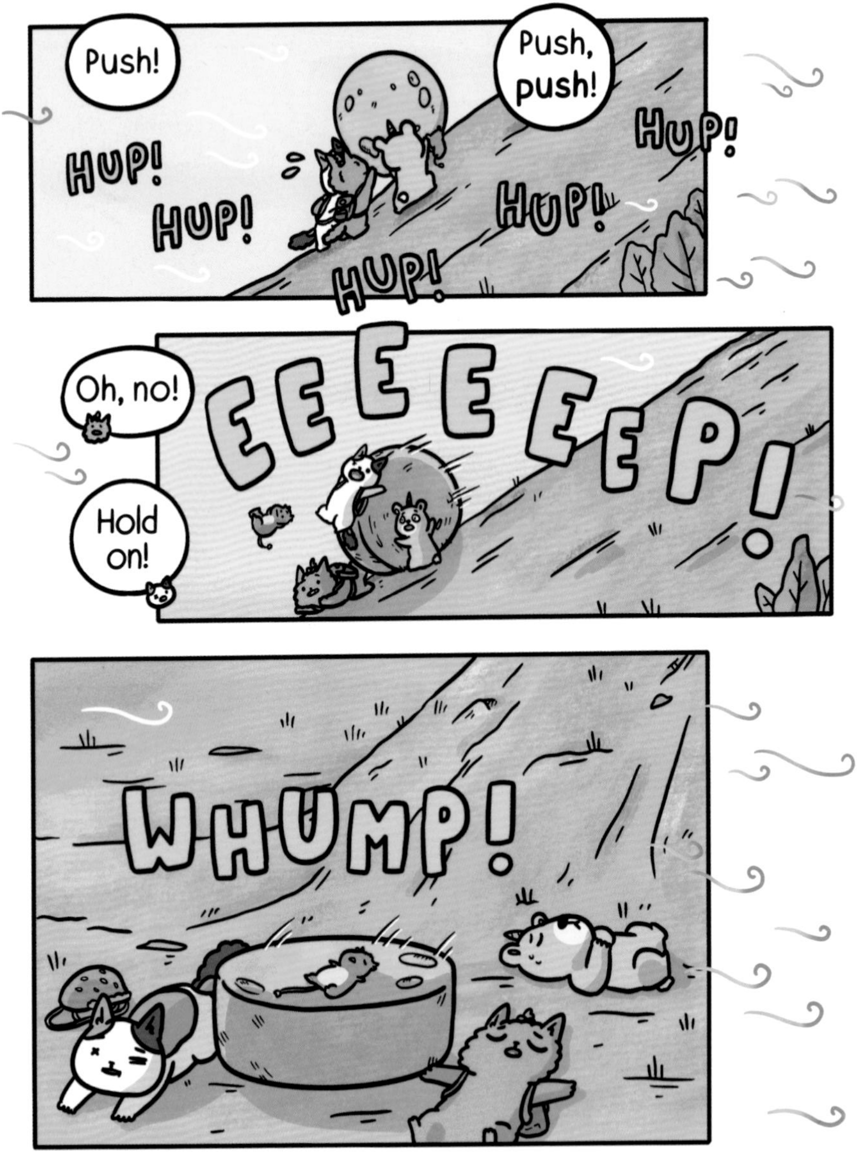
Push!
Push, push!
HUP!
HUP!
HUP!
HUP!
HUP!
Oh, no!
Hold on!
EEEEEEEP!
WHUMP!

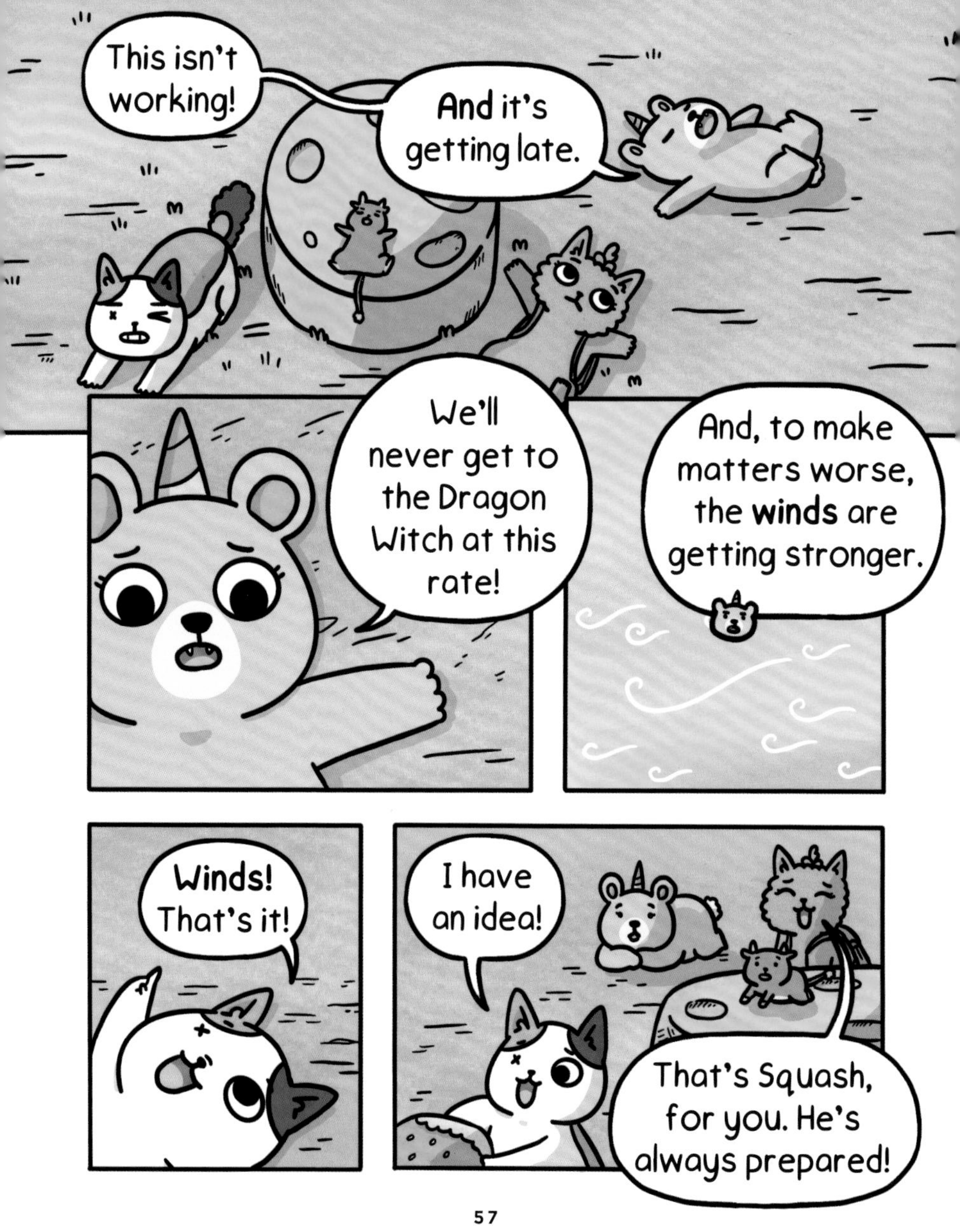
This isn't working!
And it's getting late.
We'll never get to the Dragon Witch at this rate!
And, to make matters worse, the **winds** are getting stronger.
Winds! That's it!
I have an idea!
That's Squash, for you. He's always prepared!

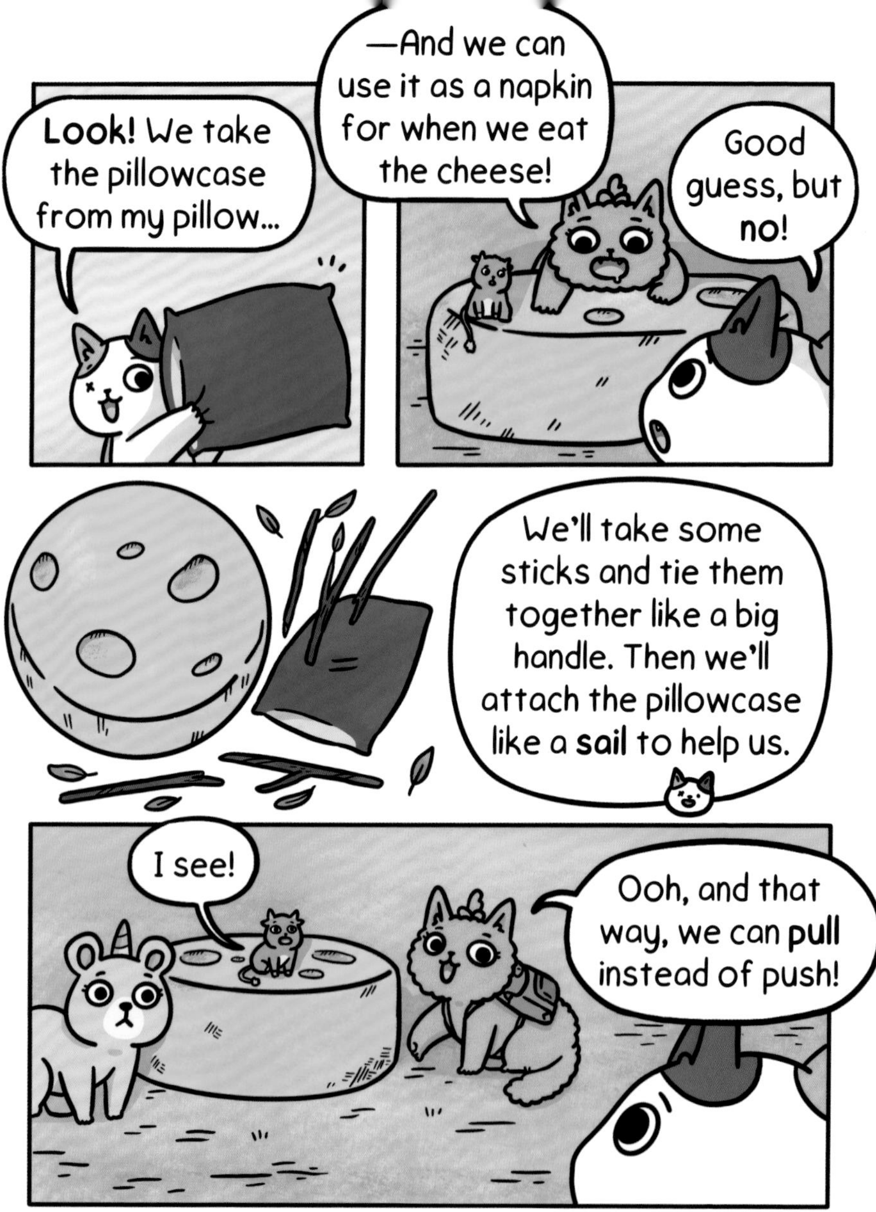
Look! We take the pillowcase from my pillow...
—And we can use it as a napkin for when we eat the cheese!
Good guess, but no!
We'll take some sticks and tie them together like a big handle. Then we'll attach the pillowcase like a sail to help us.
I see!
Ooh, and that way, we can pull instead of push!

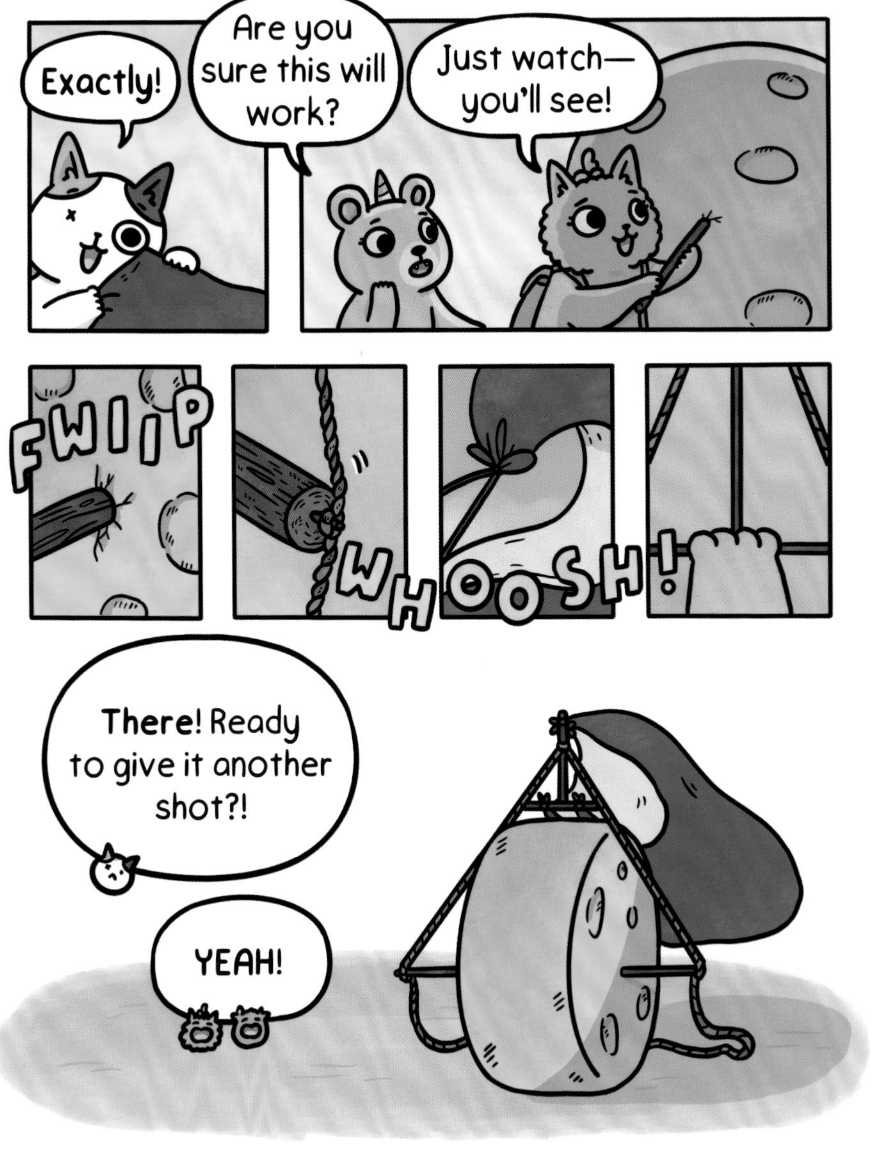
Exactly!
Are you sure this will work?
Just watch—you'll see!
FWIIP
WHOOSH!
There! Ready to give it another shot?!
YEAH!

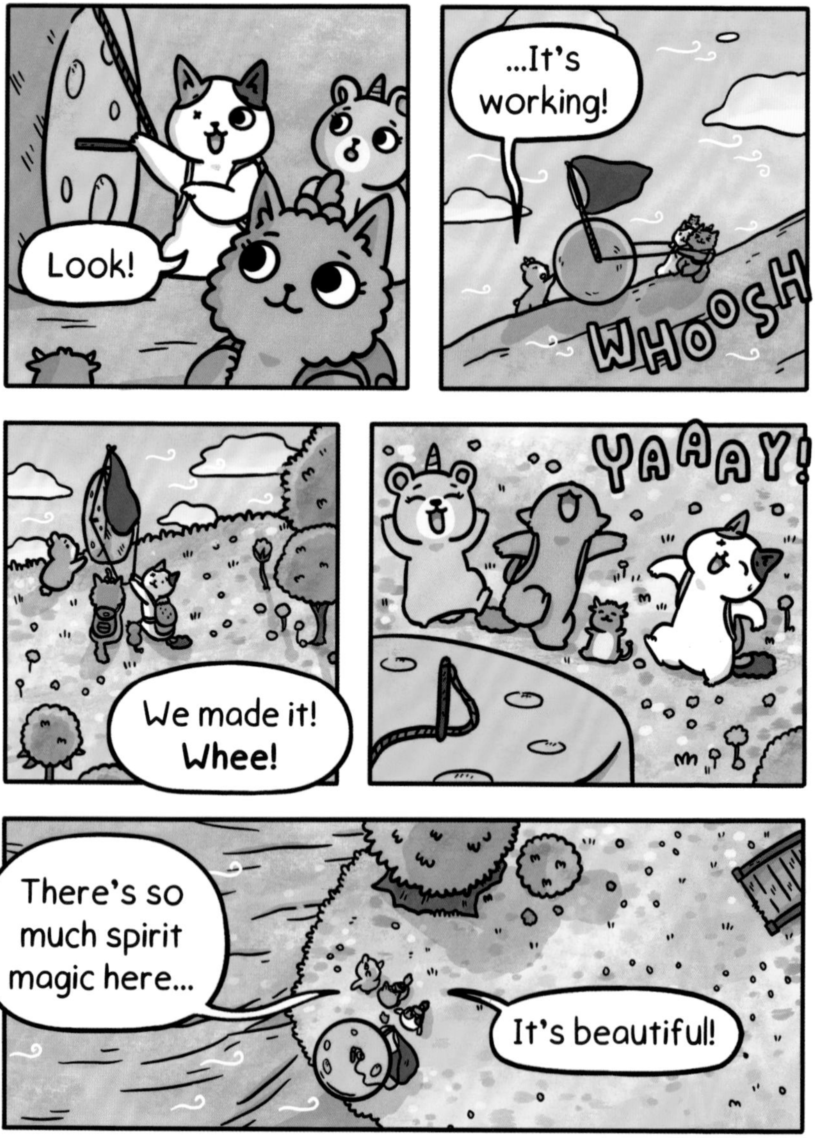
Look!
...It's working!
WHOOSH
We made it! Whee!
YAAAY!
There's so much spirit magic here...
It's beautiful!

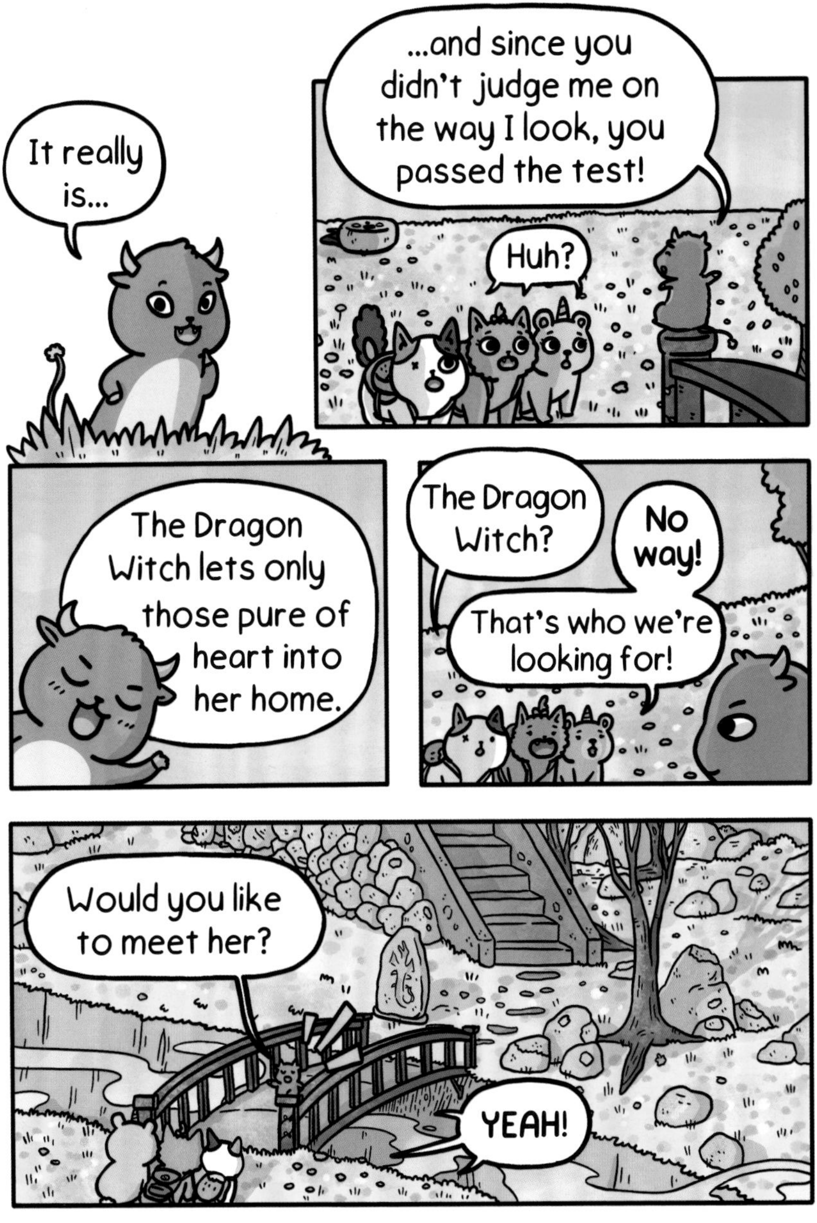
It really is...
...and since you didn't judge me on the way I look, you passed the test!
Huh?
The Dragon Witch lets only those pure of heart into her home.
The Dragon Witch?
No way!
That's who we're looking for!
Would you like to meet her?
YEAH!

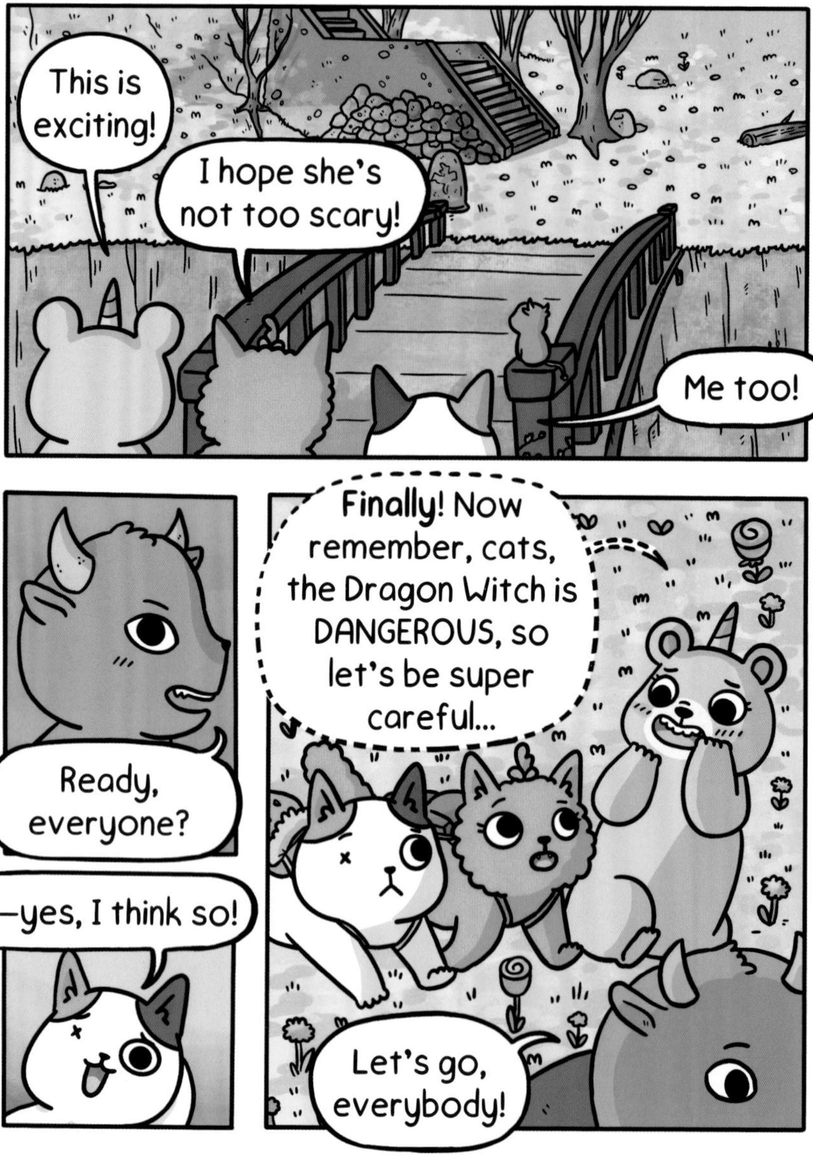
This is exciting!
I hope she's not too scary!
Me too!
Ready, everyone?
Y—yes, I think so!
Finally! Now remember, cats, the Dragon Witch is DANGEROUS, so let's be super careful...
Let's go, everybody!

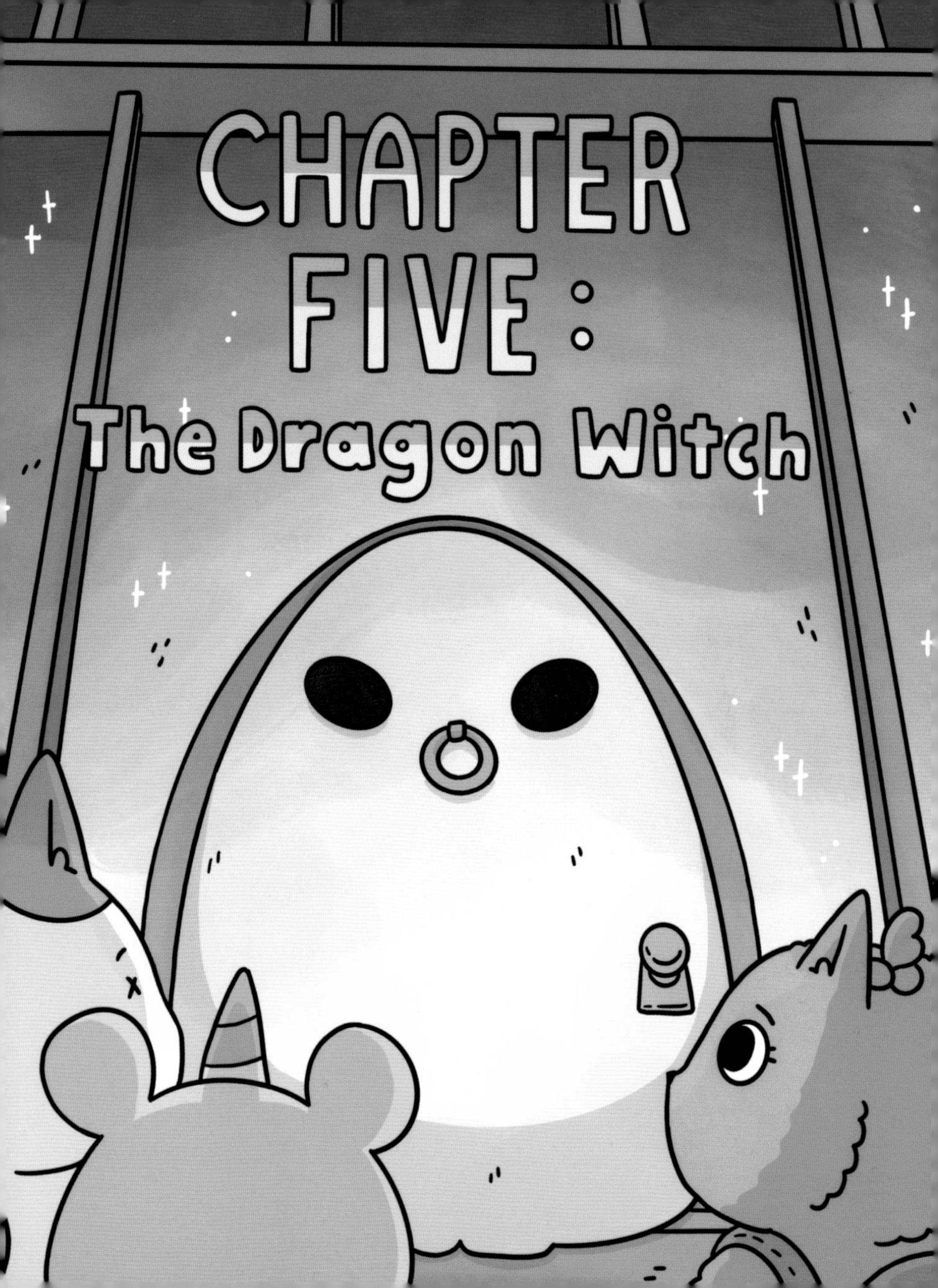
CHAPTER FIVE:
The Dragon Witch

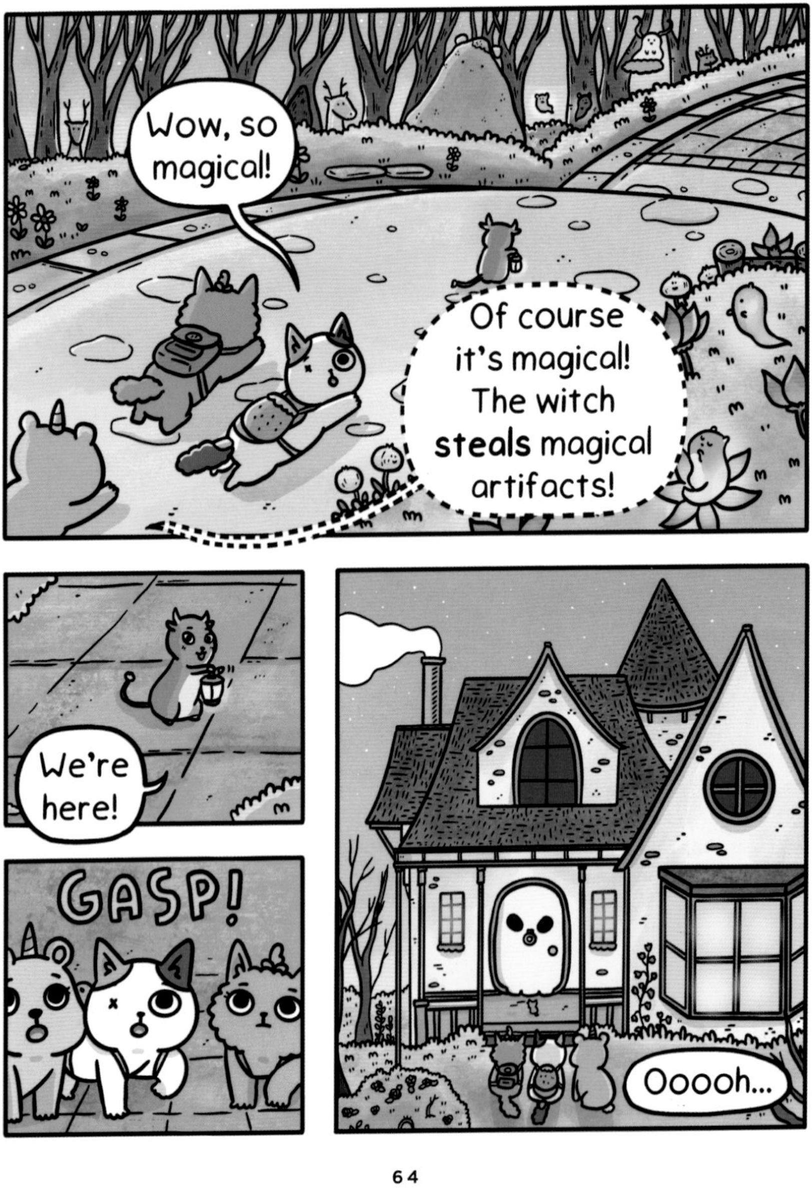
Wow, so magical!
Of course it's magical! The witch **steals** magical artifacts!
We're here!
GASP!
Ooooh...

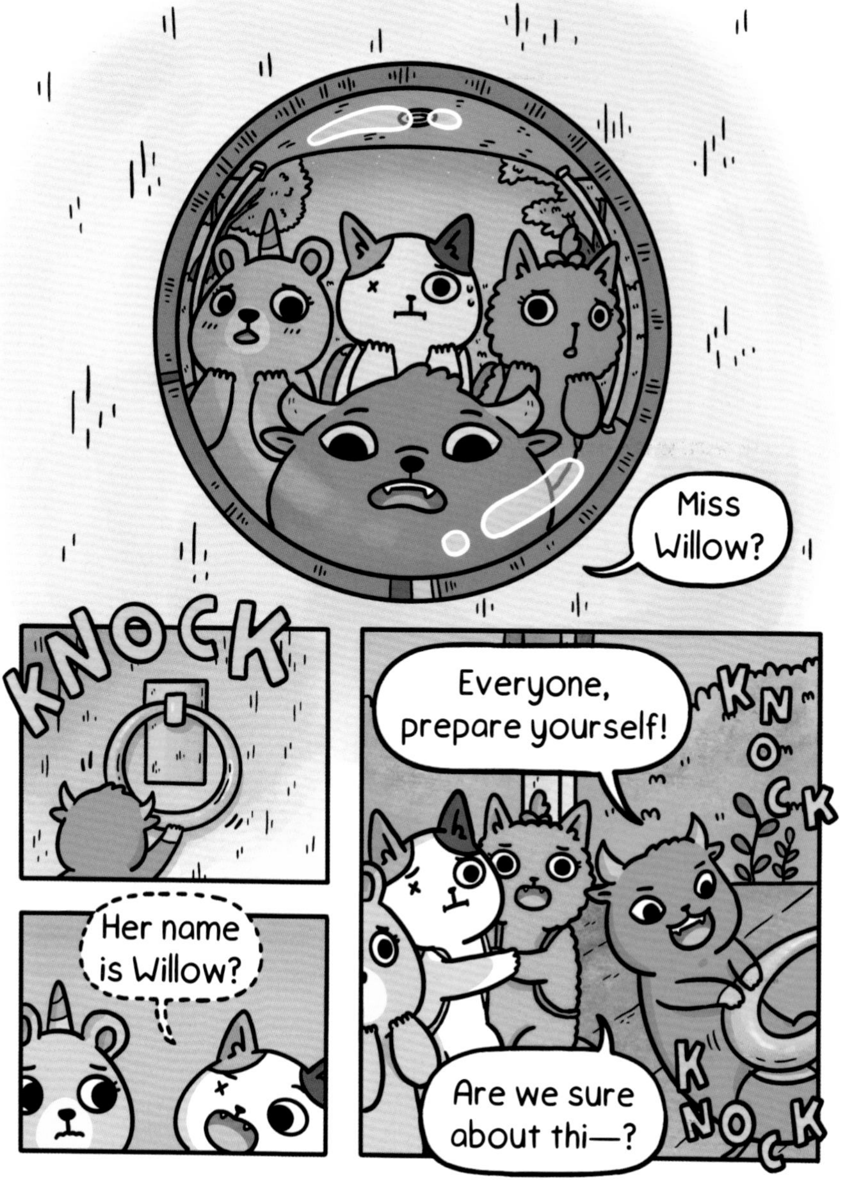
Miss Willow?
KNOCK
Her name is Willow?
Everyone, prepare yourself!
KNOCK
KNOCK
Are we sure about thi—?

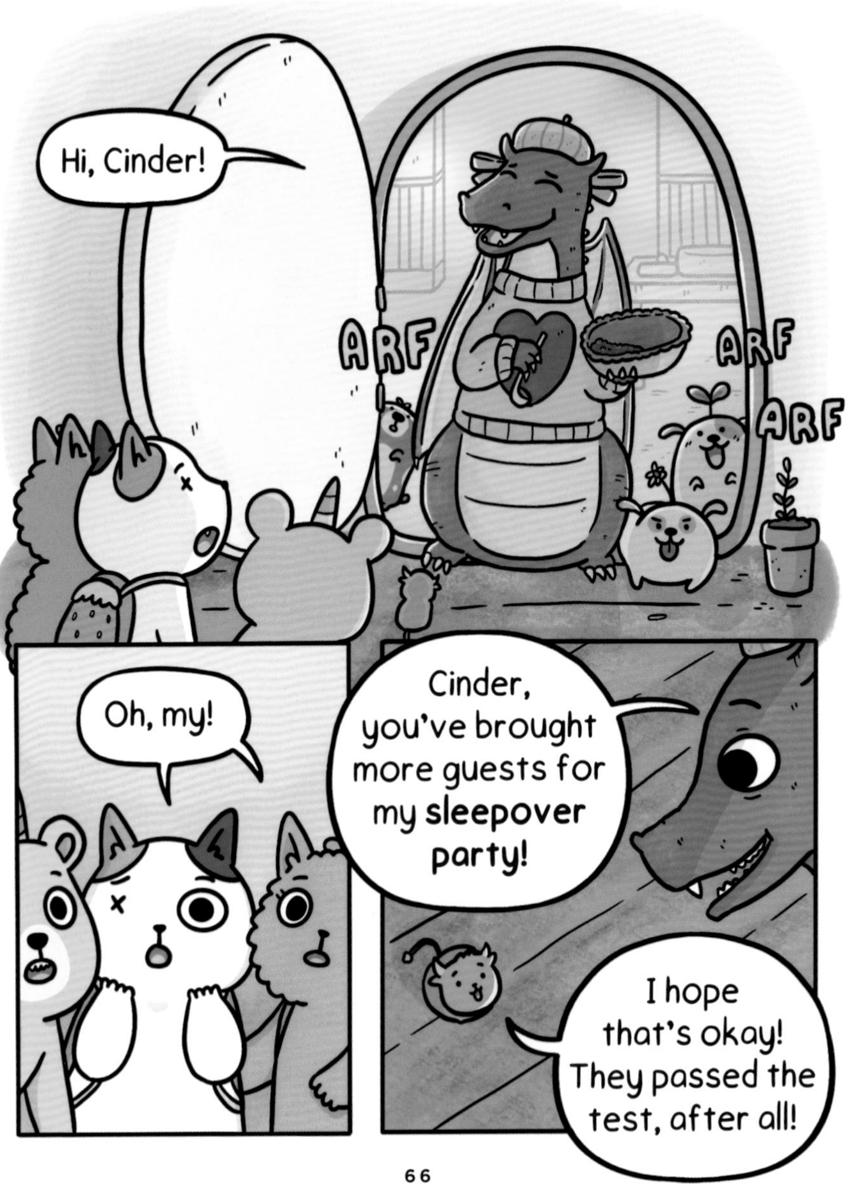
Hi, Cinder!
ARF
ARF
ARF
Oh, my!
Cinder, you've brought more guests for my **sleepover party!**
I hope that's okay! They passed the test, after all!

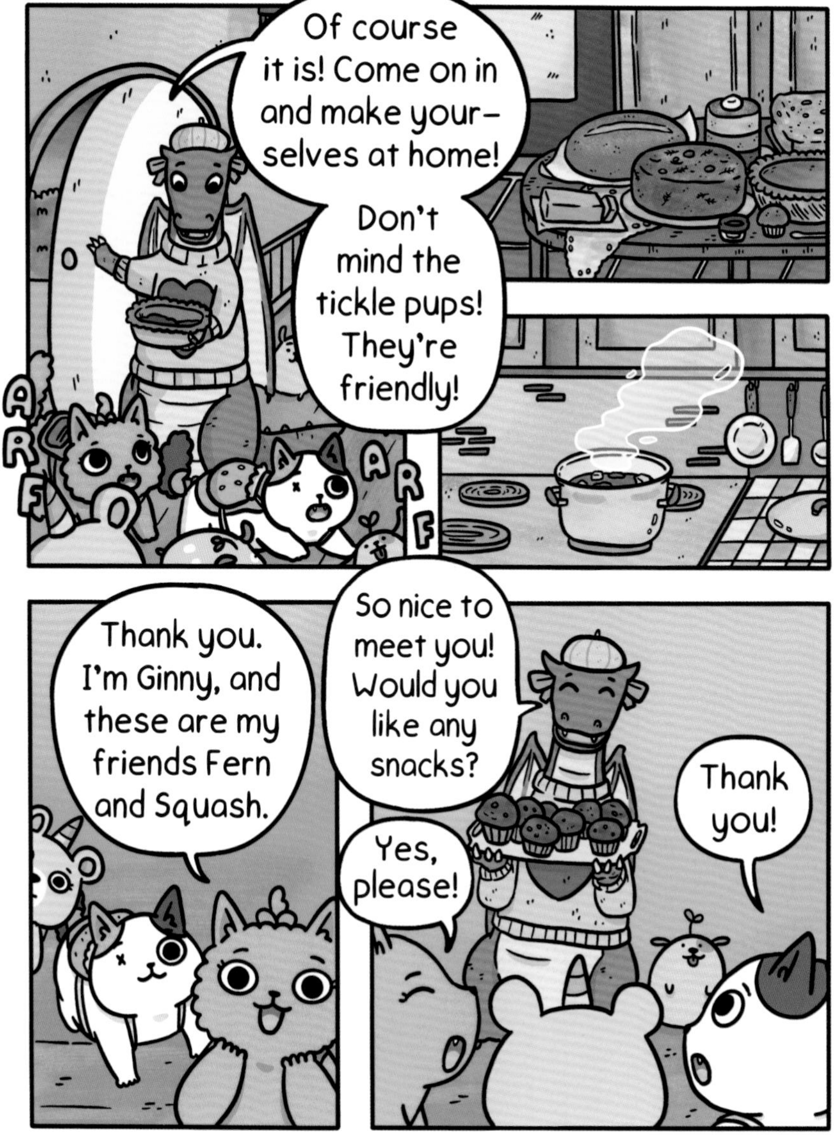

Of course it is! Come on in and make your-selves at home!
Don't mind the tickle pups! They're friendly!
ARF
ARF
Thank you. I'm Ginny, and these are my friends Fern and Squash.
So nice to meet you! Would you like any snacks?
Yes, please!
Thank you!

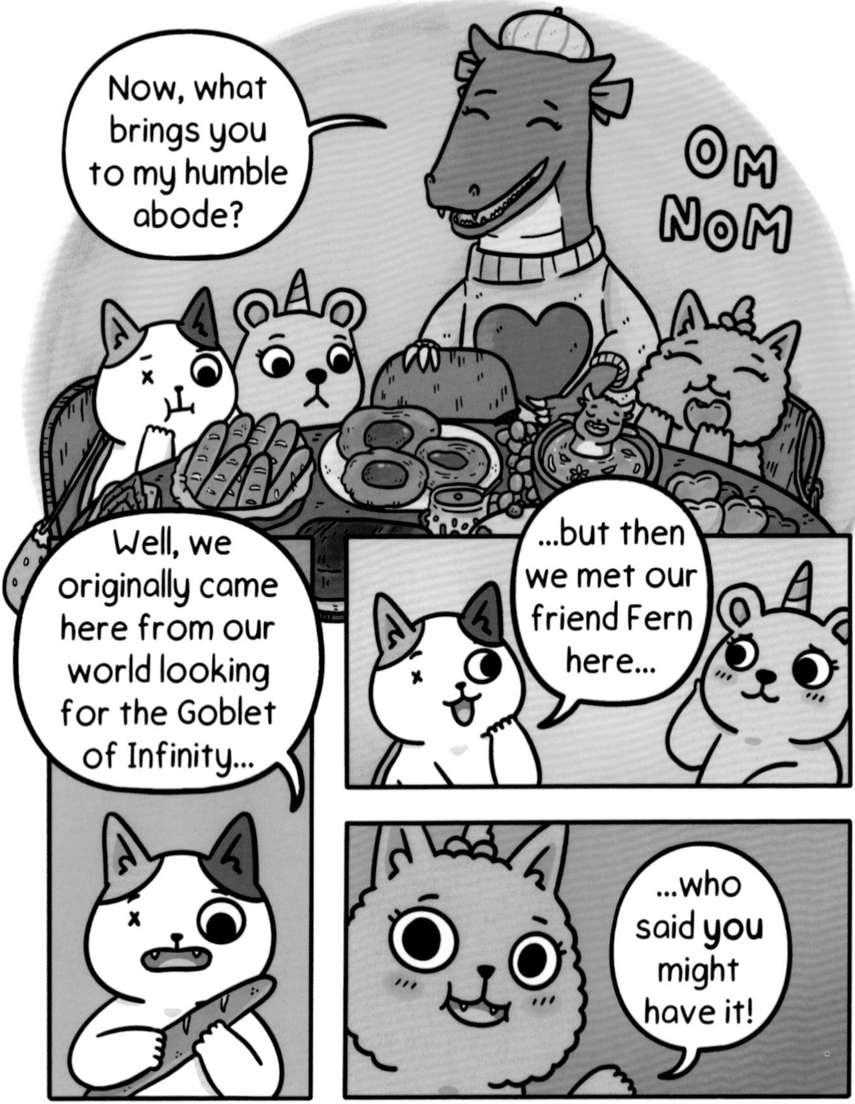
Now, what brings you to my humble abode?
OM NOM
Well, we originally came here from our world looking for the Goblet of Infinity...
...but then we met our friend Fern here...
...who said **you** might have it!

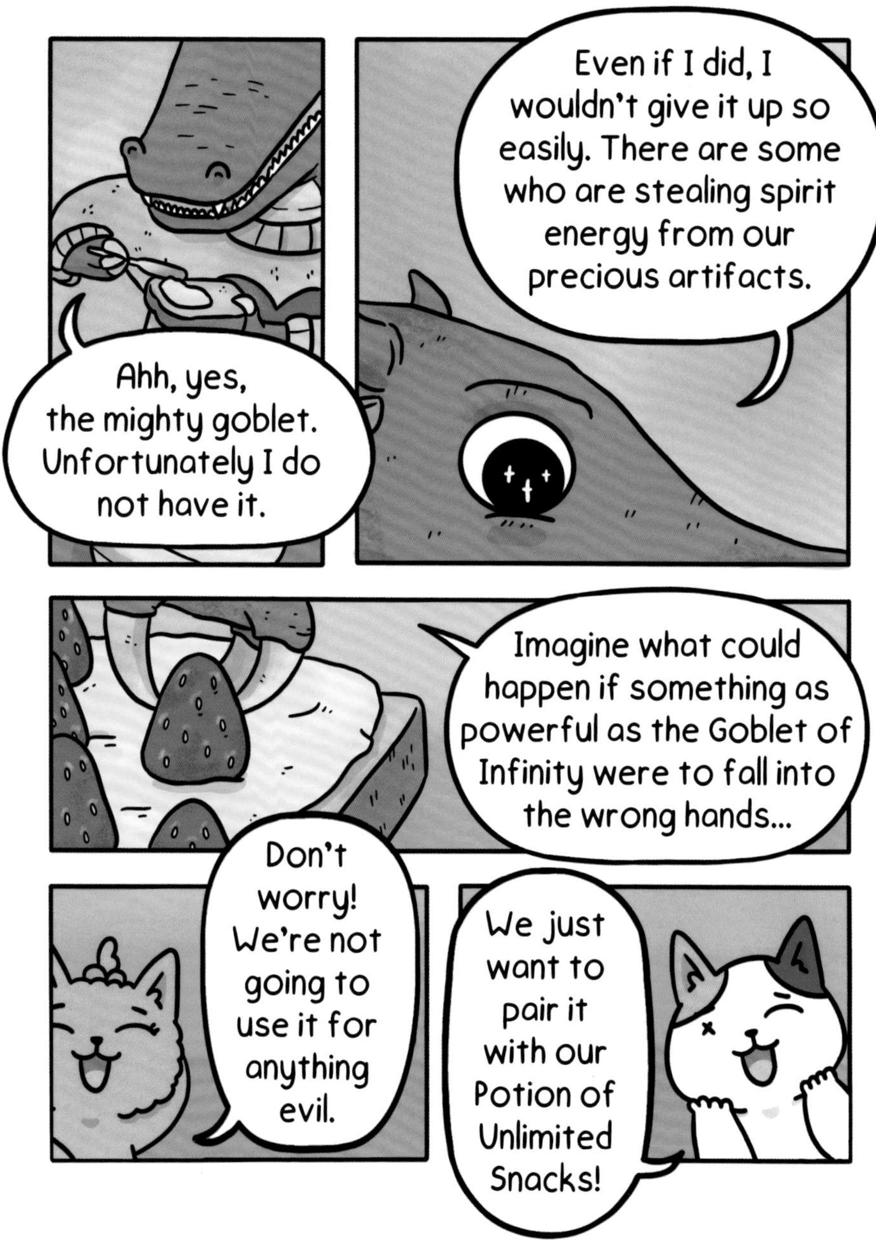
Ahh, yes, the mighty goblet. Unfortunately I do not have it.
Even if I did, I wouldn't give it up so easily. There are some who are stealing spirit energy from our precious artifacts.
Imagine what could happen if something as powerful as the Goblet of Infinity were to fall into the wrong hands...
Don't worry! We're not going to use it for anything evil.
We just want to pair it with our Potion of Unlimited Snacks!

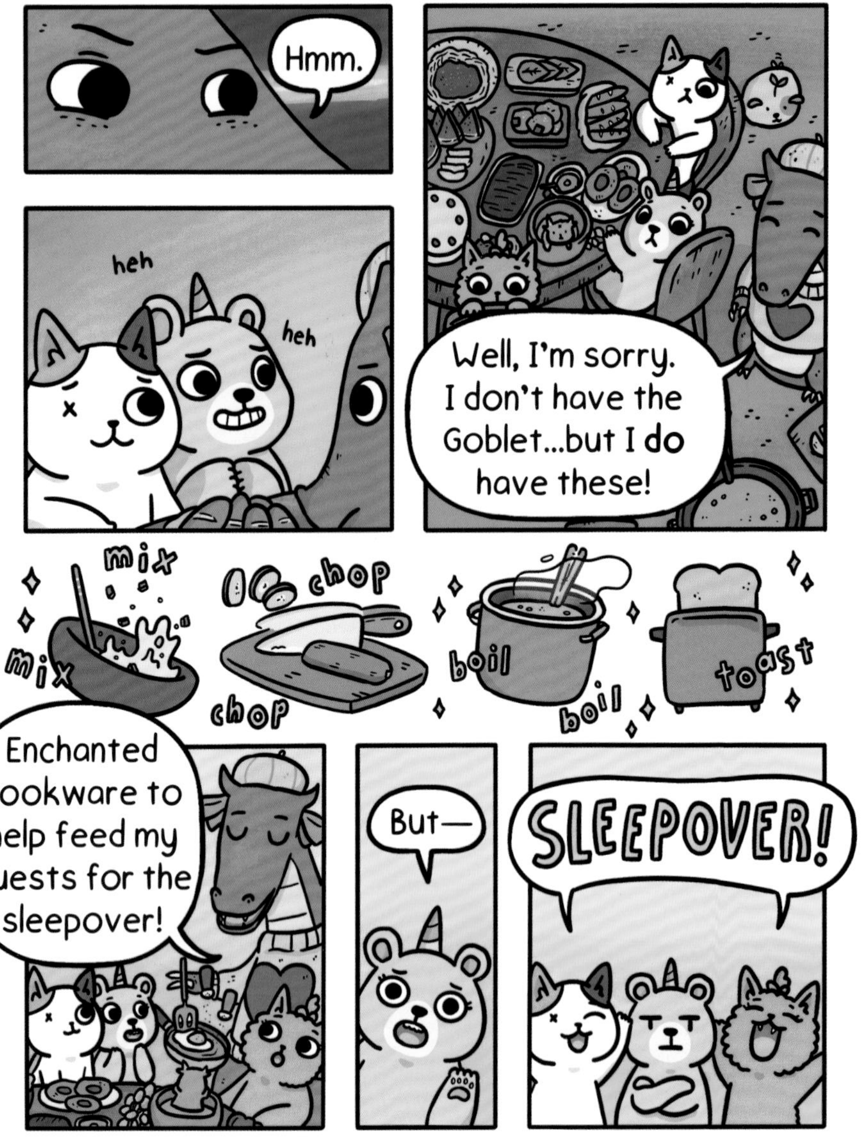
Hmm.
heh
heh
Well, I'm sorry. I don't have the Goblet...but I do have these!
mix
mix
chop
chop
boil
boil
toast
Enchanted cookware to help feed my guests for the sleepover!
But—
SLEEPOVER!

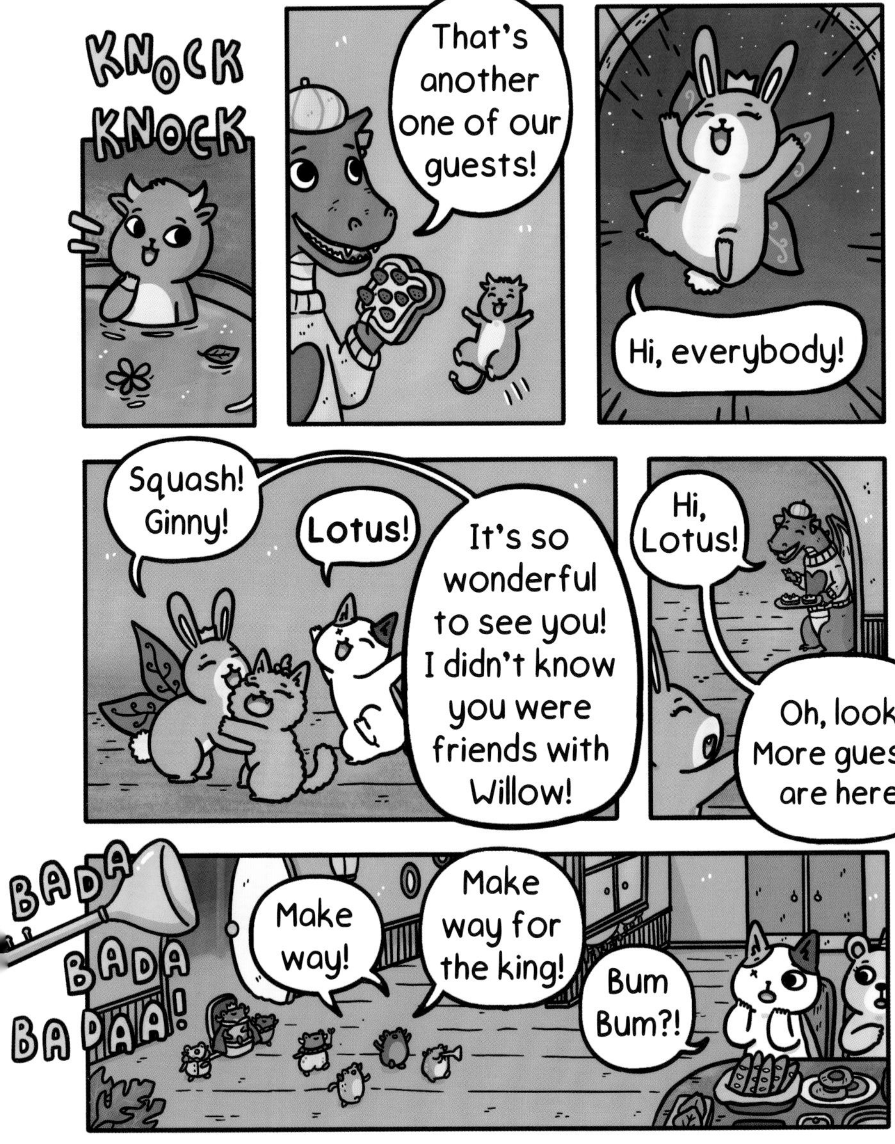
KNOCK KNOCK
That's another one of our guests!
Hi, everybody!
Squash! Ginny!
Lotus!
It's so wonderful to see you! I didn't know you were friends with Willow!
Hi, Lotus!
Oh, look! More guests are here!
BADA BADA BADAA!
Make way!
Make way for the king!
Bum Bum?!

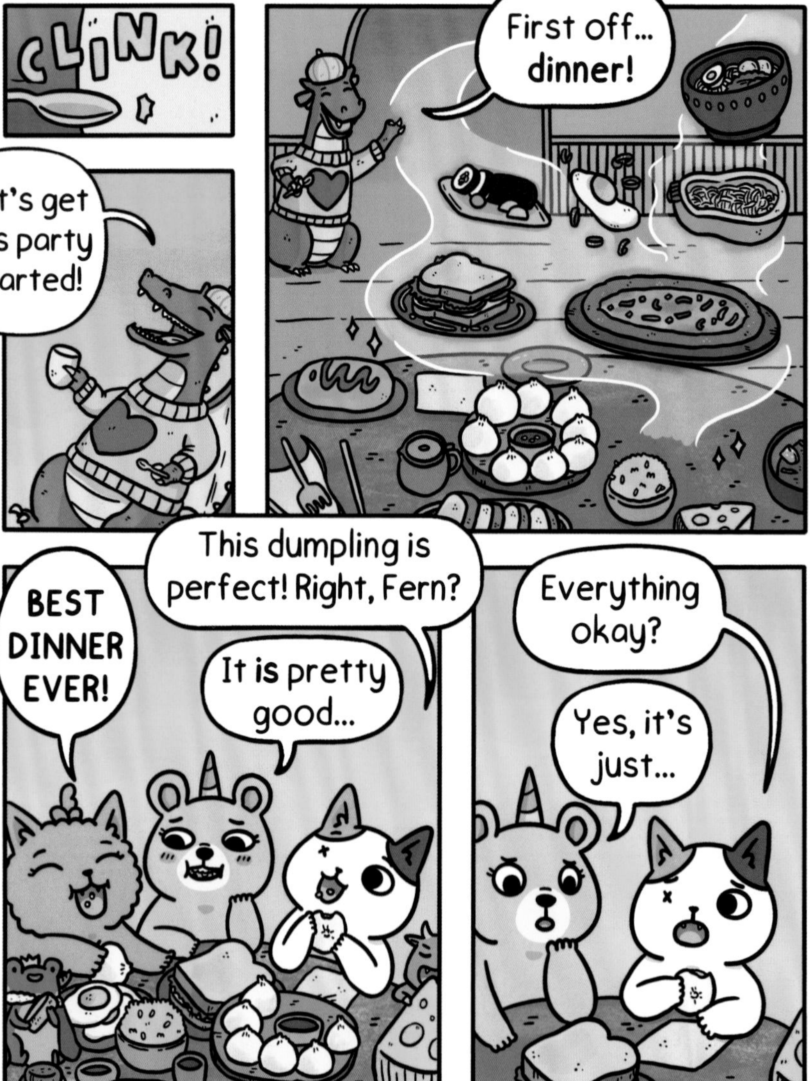
CLINK!
Let's get this party started!
First off... dinner!
BEST DINNER EVER!
This dumpling is perfect! Right, Fern?
It **is** pretty good...
Everything okay?
Yes, it's just...

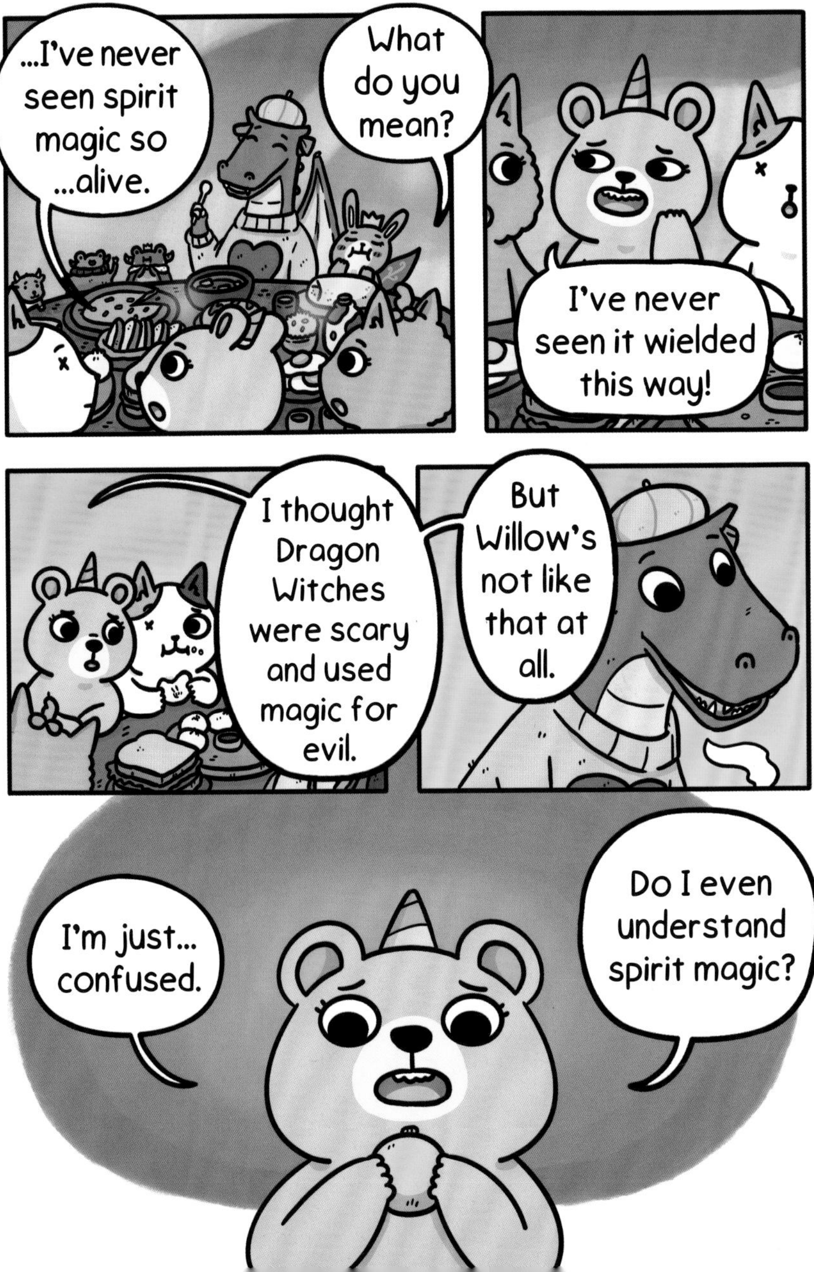
...I've never seen spirit magic so ...alive.
What do you mean?
I've never seen it wielded this way!
I thought Dragon Witches were scary and used magic for evil.
But Willow's not like that at all.
I'm just... confused.
Do I even understand spirit magic?

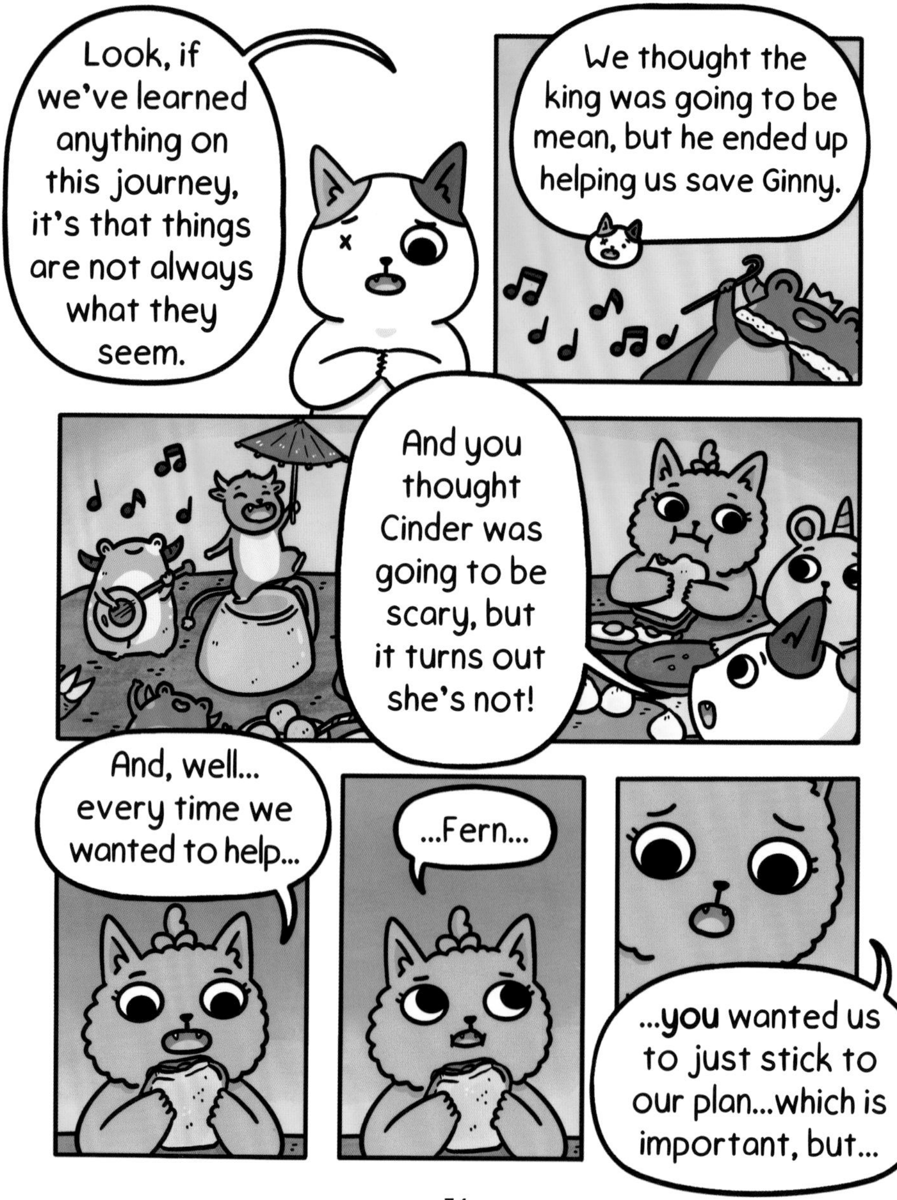

Look, if we've learned anything on this journey, it's that things are not always what they seem.
We thought the king was going to be mean, but he ended up helping us save Ginny.
And you thought Cinder was going to be scary, but it turns out she's not!
And, well... every time we wanted to help...
...Fern...
...**you** wanted us to just stick to our plan...which is important, but...

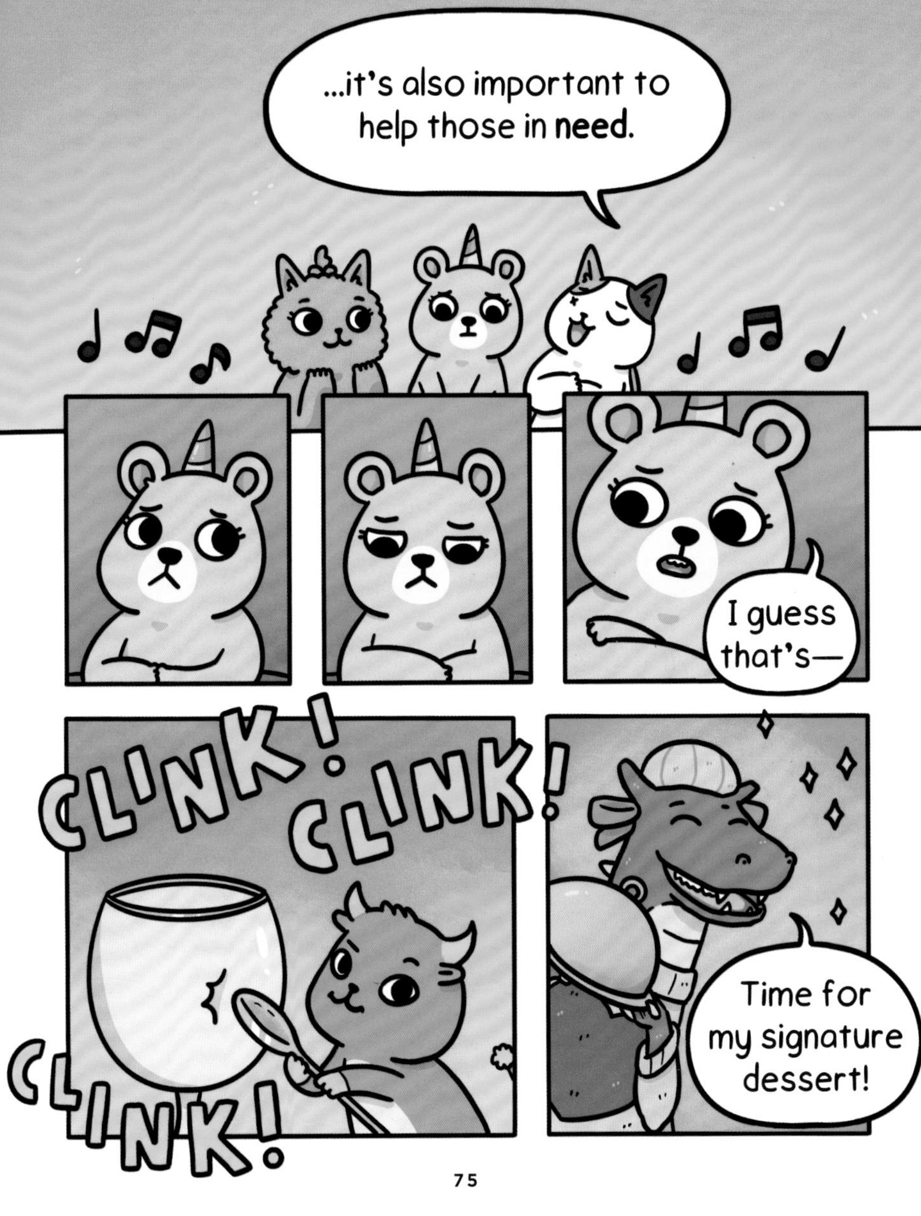
...it's also important to help those in **need**.
I guess that's—
CLINK! CLINK!
CLINK!
Time for my signature dessert!

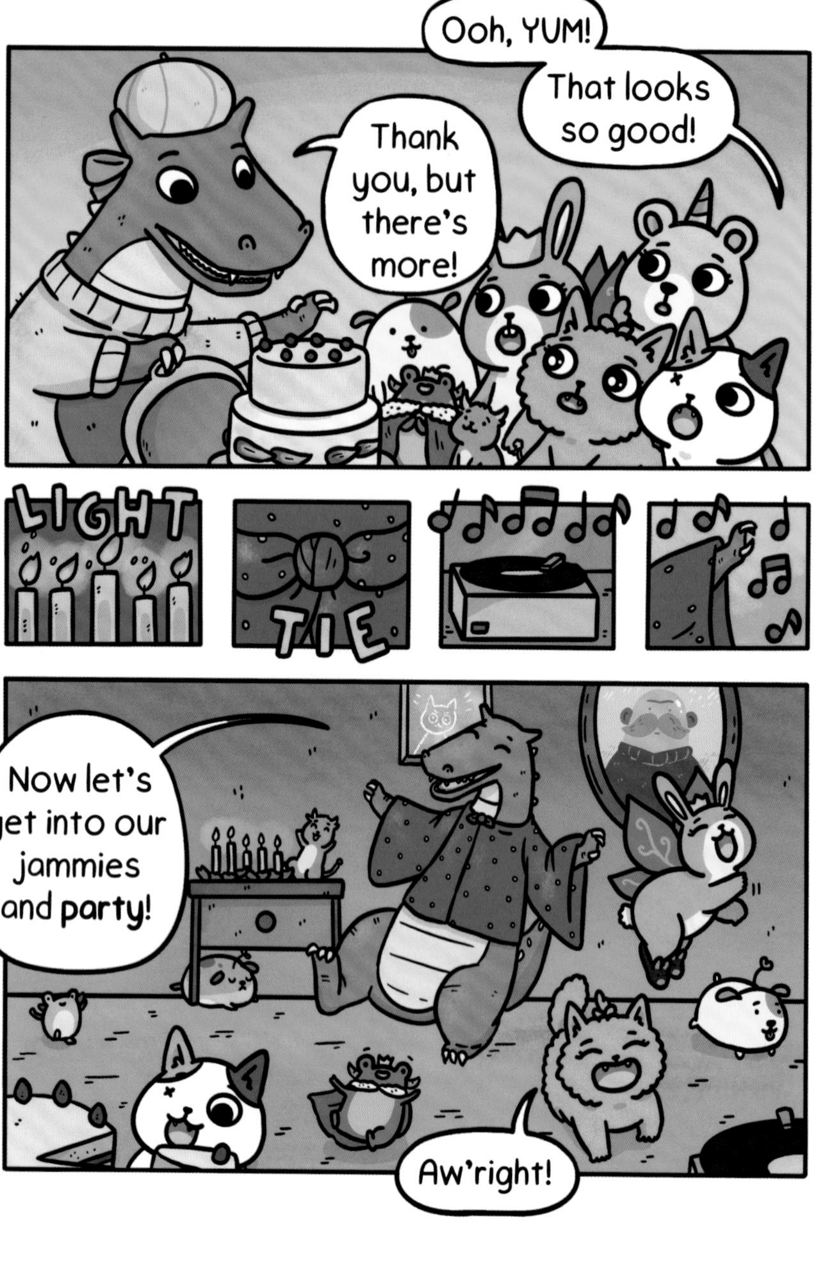
Ooh, YUM!
That looks so good!
Thank you, but there's more!
LIGHT
TIE
Now let's get into our jammies and **party**!
Aw'right!

CHAPTER SIX:
The Truth

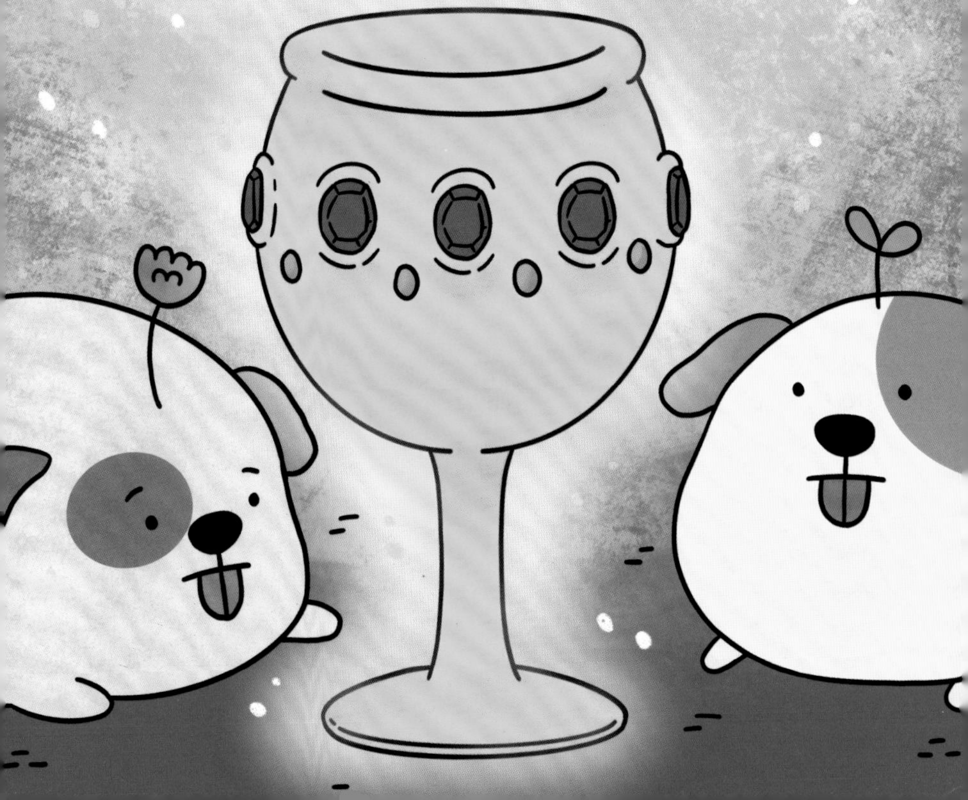

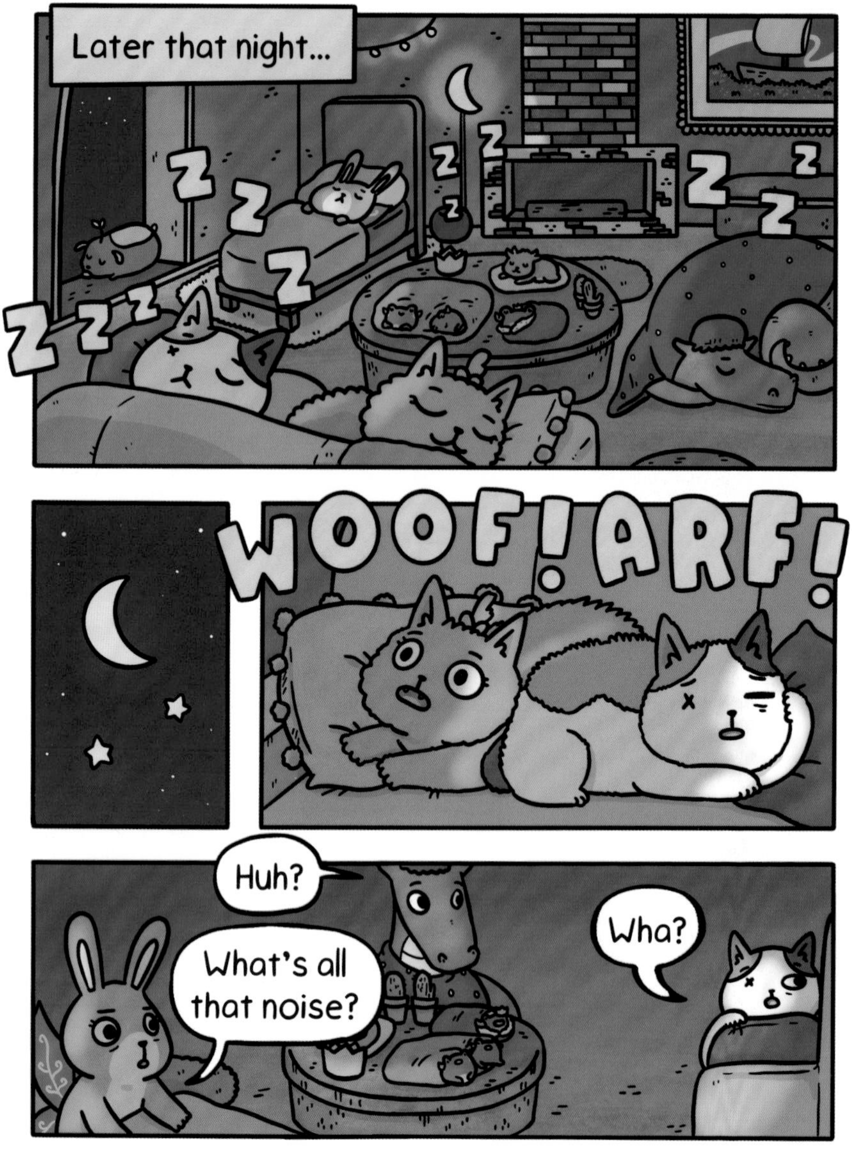

Later that night...
Z Z Z
Z Z Z
Z Z
Z Z
Z
WOOF! ARF!
Huh?
What's all that noise?
Wha?

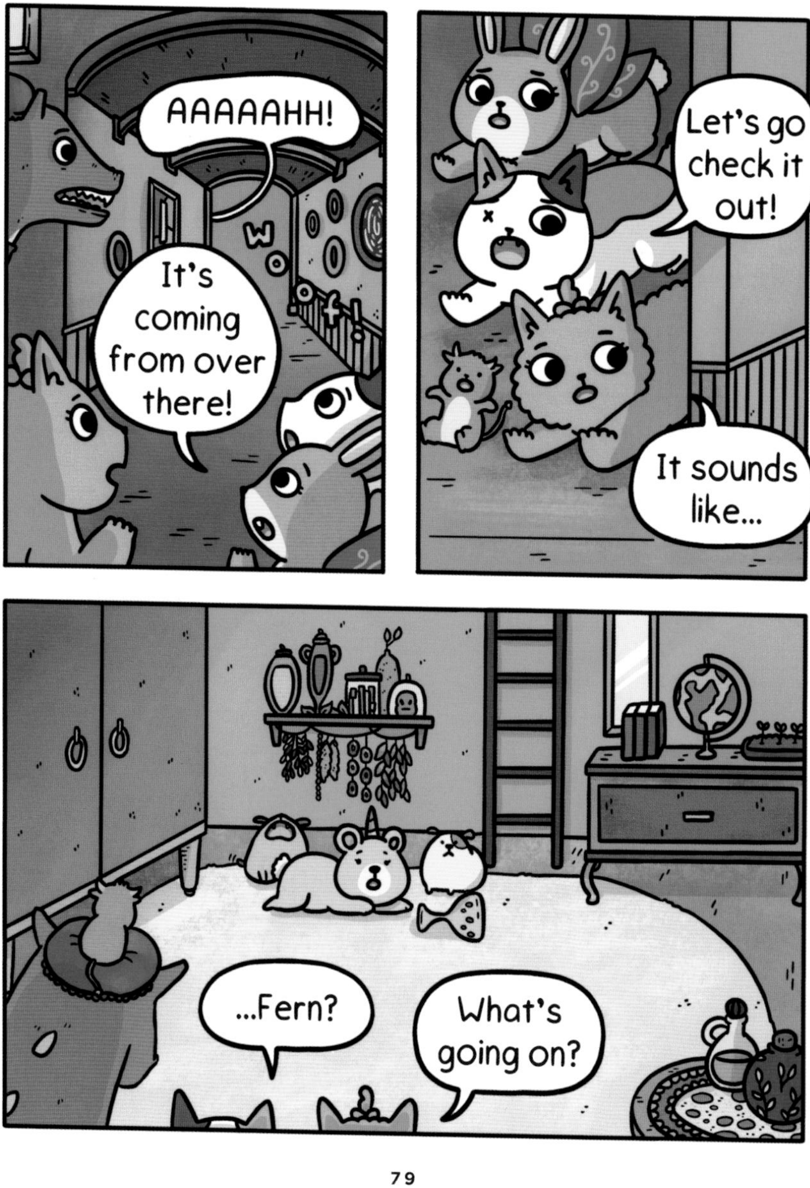
AAAAAHH!
It's coming from over there!
Let's go check it out!
It sounds like...
...Fern?
What's going on?

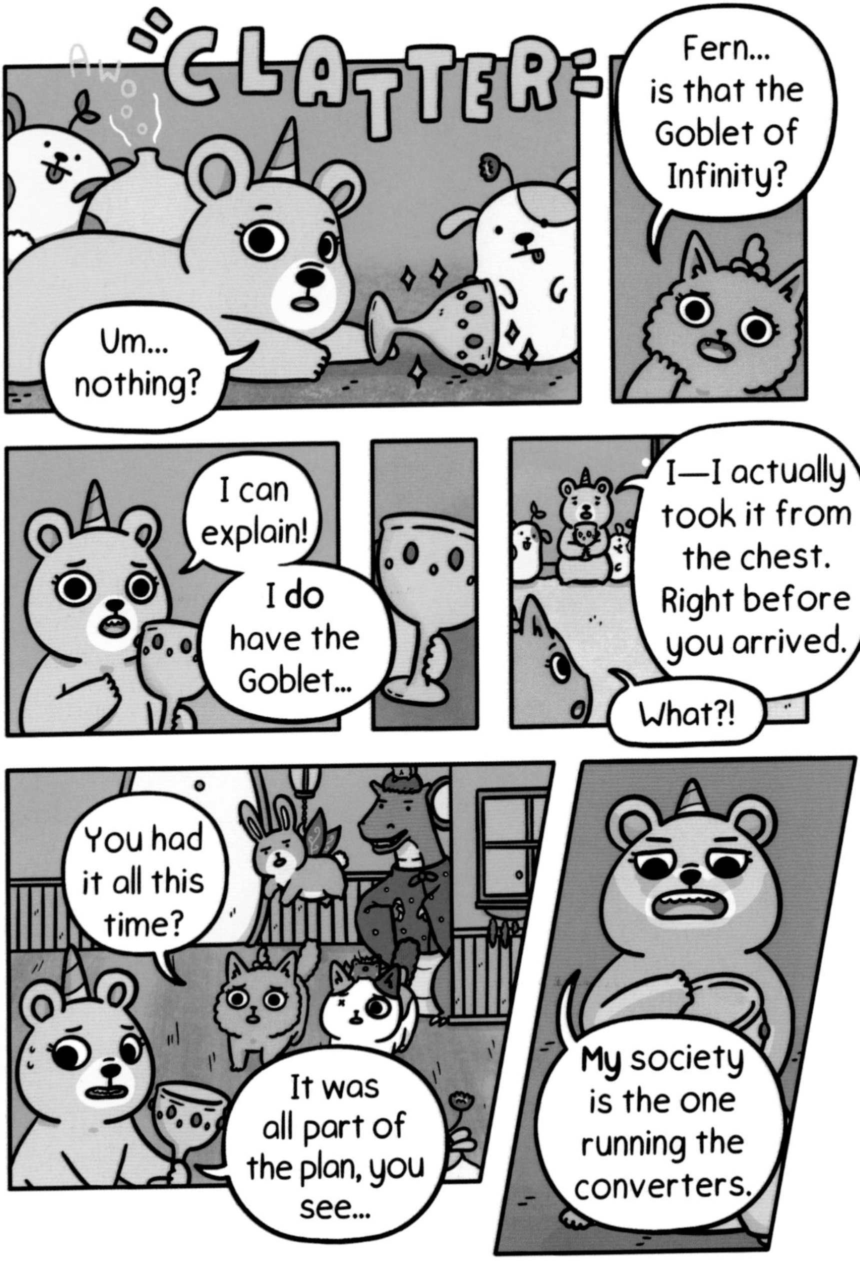
AWOO
CLATTER
Um... nothing?
Fern... is that the Goblet of Infinity?
I can explain!
I do have the Goblet...
I—I actually took it from the chest. Right before you arrived.
What?!
You had it all this time?
It was all part of the plan, you see...
My society is the one running the converters.

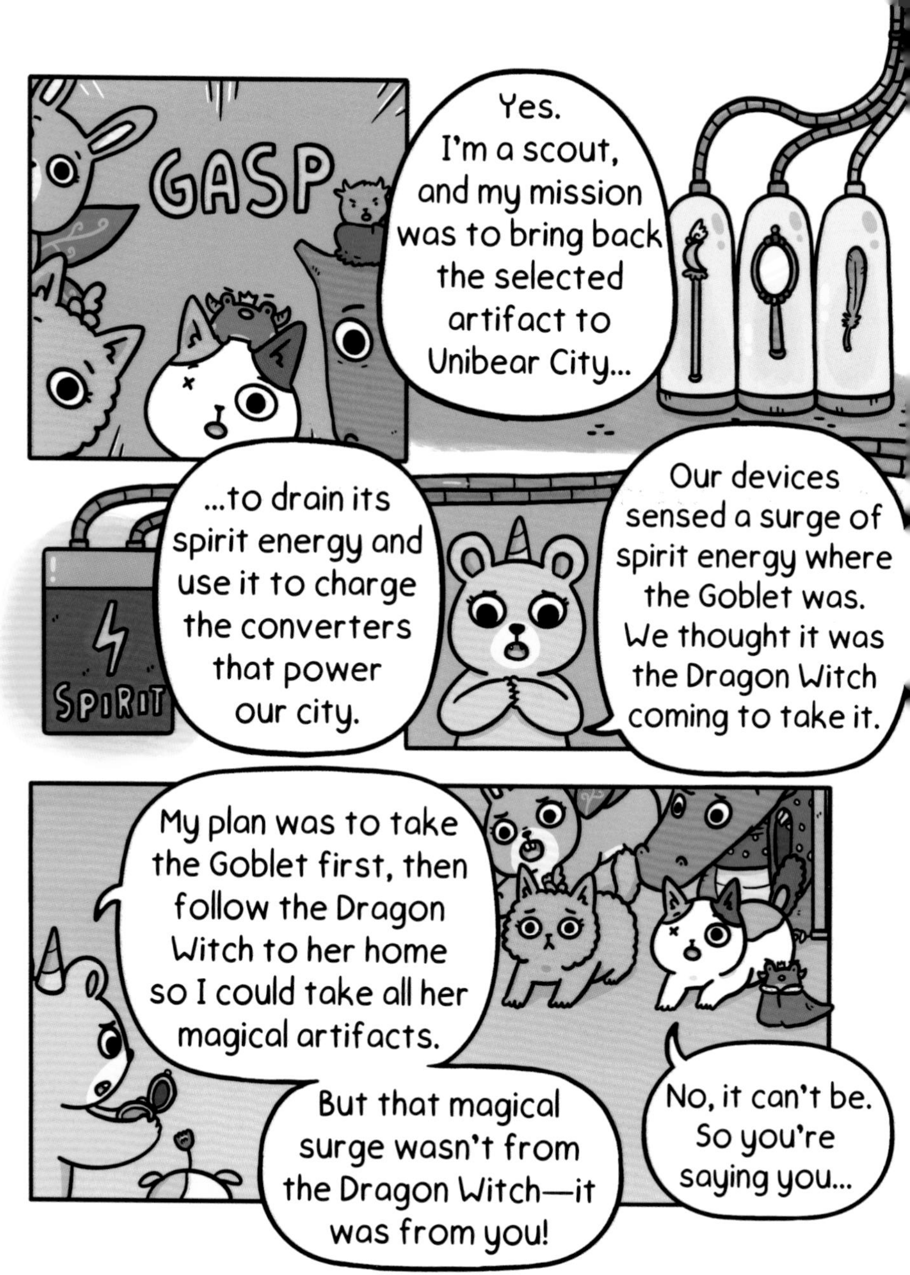
GASP
Yes. I'm a scout, and my mission was to bring back the selected artifact to Unibear City...
...to drain its spirit energy and use it to charge the converters that power our city.
SPIRIT
Our devices sensed a surge of spirit energy where the Goblet was. We thought it was the Dragon Witch coming to take it.
My plan was to take the Goblet first, then follow the Dragon Witch to her home so I could take all her magical artifacts.
But that magical surge wasn't from the Dragon Witch—it was from you!
No, it can't be. So you're saying you...

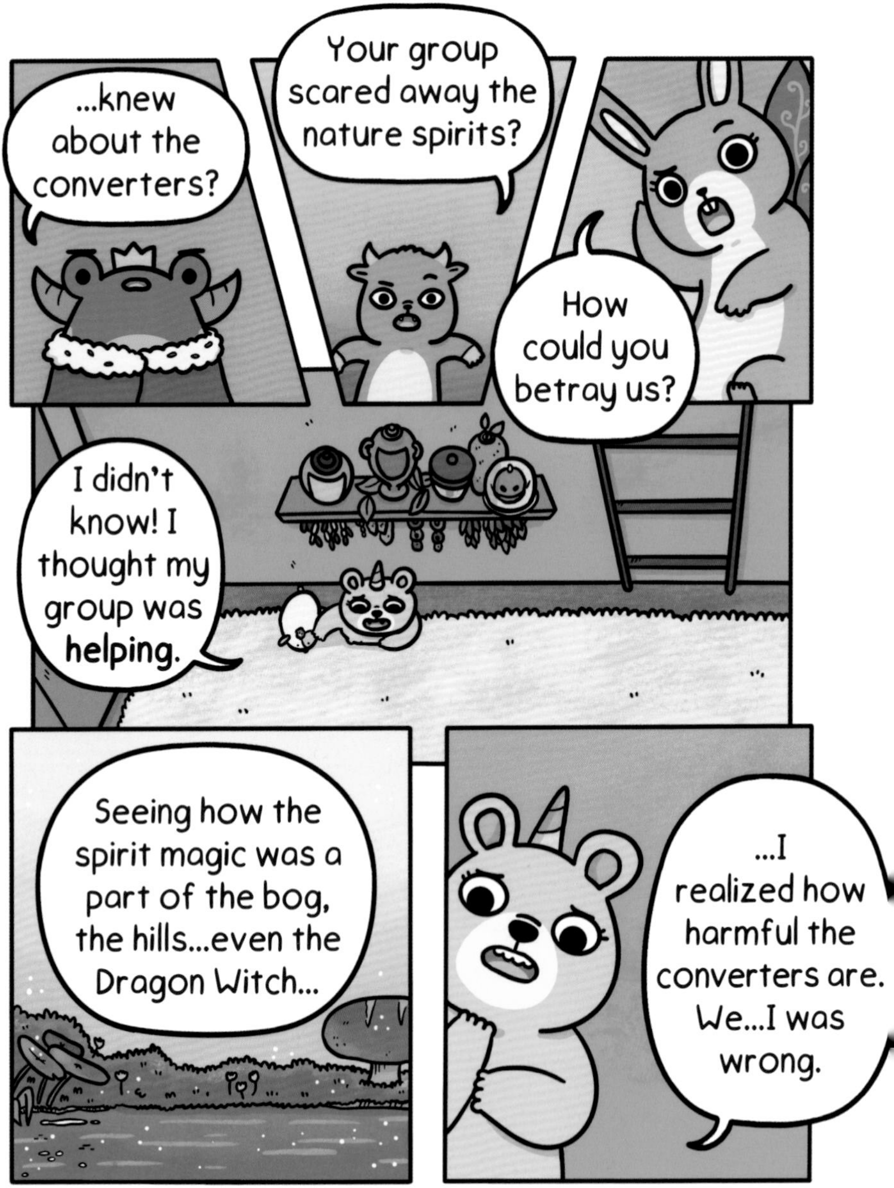
...knew about the converters?
Your group scared away the nature spirits?
How could you betray us?
I didn't know! I thought my group was **helping**.
Seeing how the spirit magic was a part of the bog, the hills...even the Dragon Witch...
...I realized how harmful the converters are. We...I was wrong.

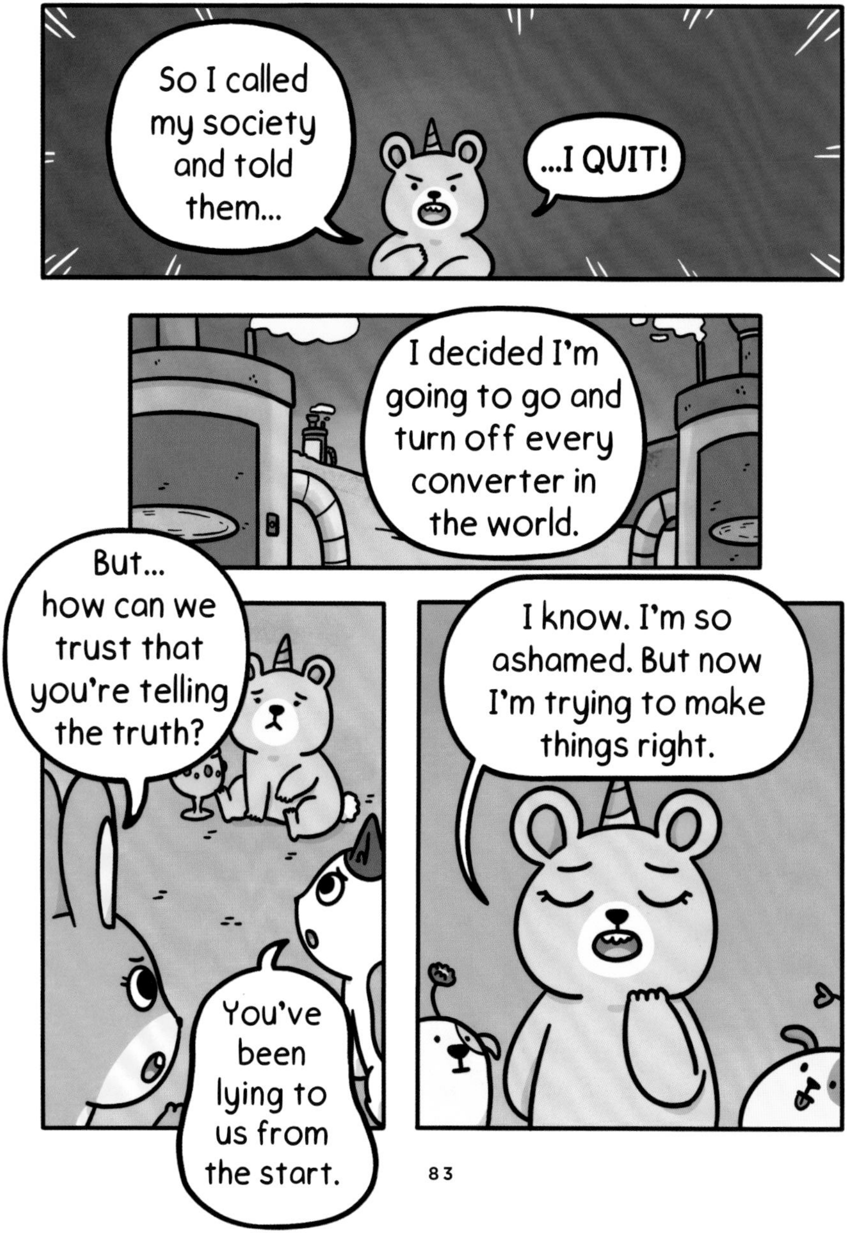
So I called my society and told them...
...I QUIT!
I decided I'm going to go and turn off every converter in the world.
But... how can we trust that you're telling the truth?
You've been lying to us from the start.
I know. I'm so ashamed. But now I'm trying to make things right.

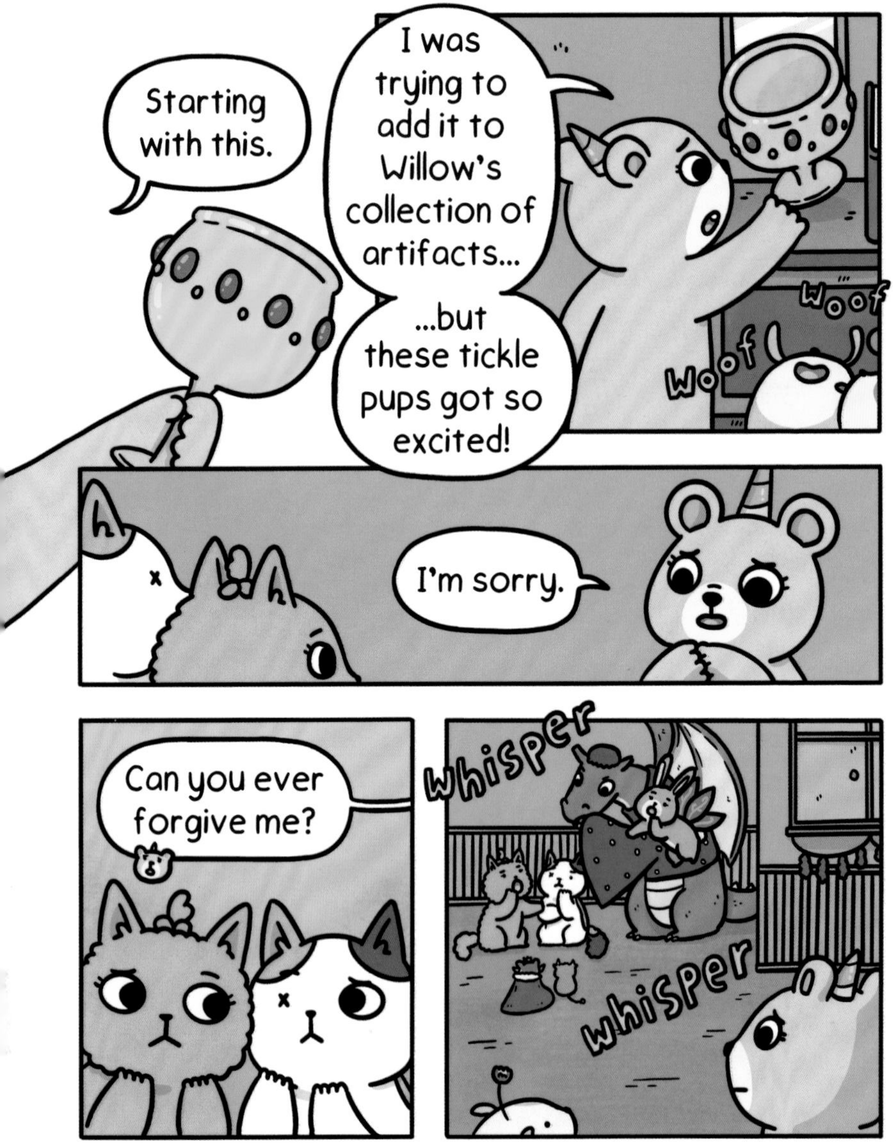
Starting with this.
I was trying to add it to Willow's collection of artifacts...
...but these tickle pups got so excited!
Woof
Woof
I'm sorry.
Can you ever forgive me?
whisper
whisper

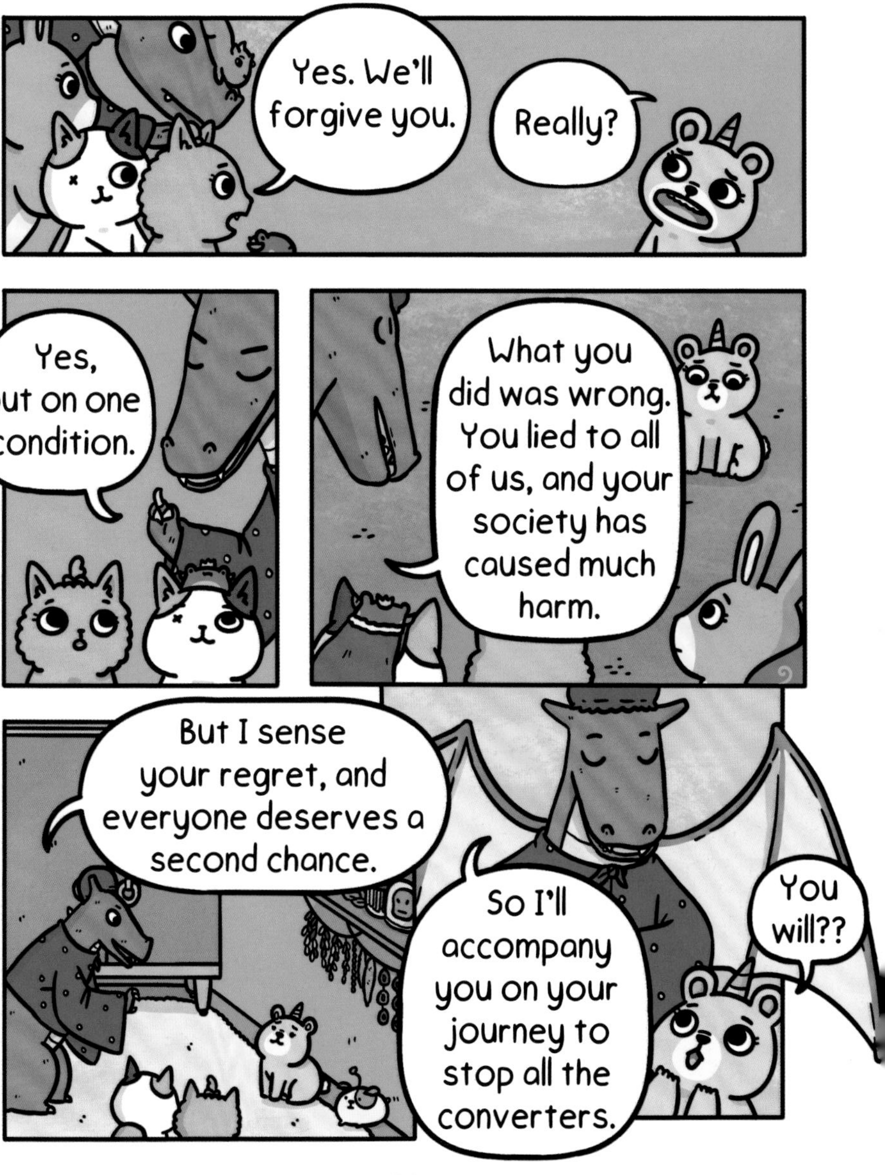
Yes. We'll forgive you.
Really?
Yes, but on one condition.
What you did was wrong. You lied to all of us, and your society has caused much harm.
But I sense your regret, and everyone deserves a second chance.
So I'll accompany you on your journey to stop all the converters.
You will??

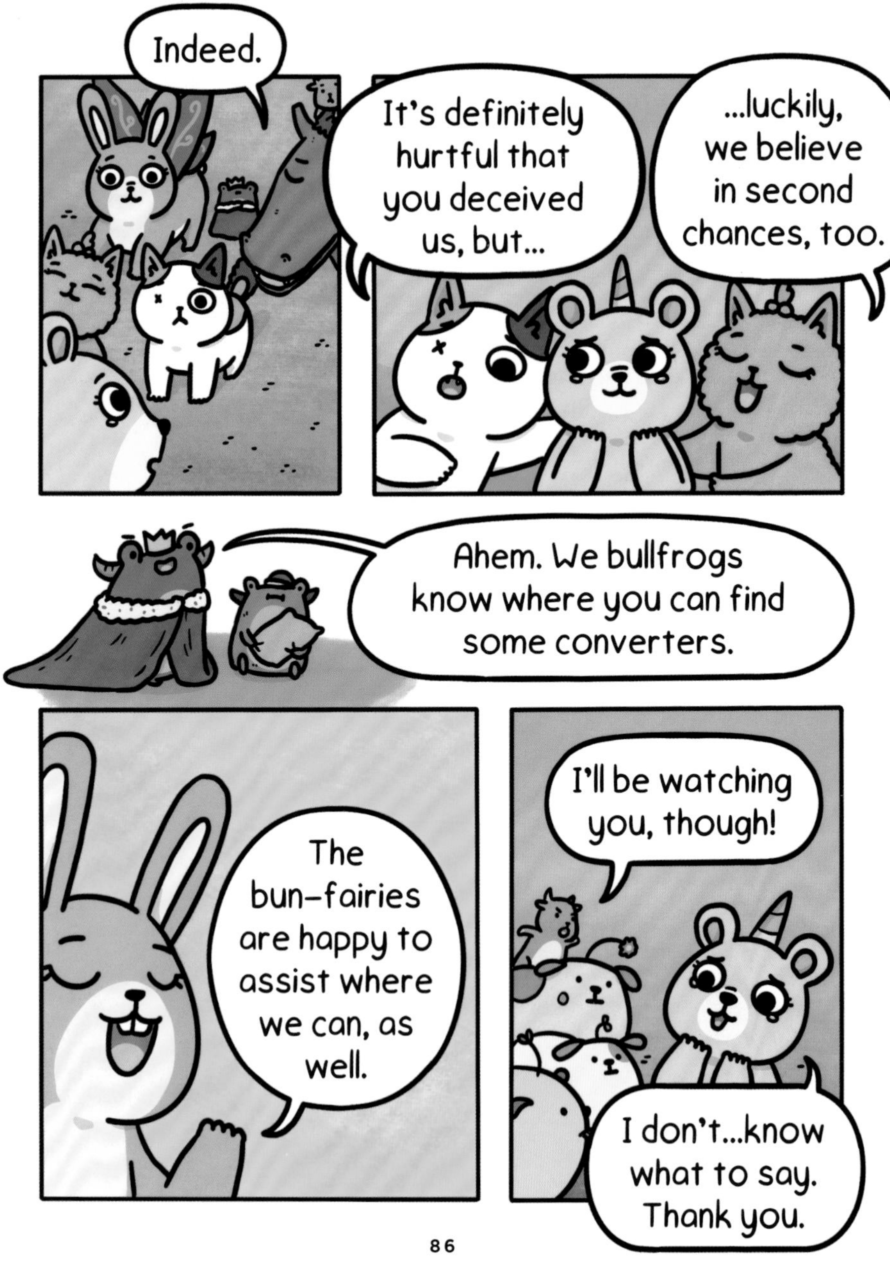
Indeed.
It's definitely hurtful that you deceived us, but...
...luckily, we believe in second chances, too.
Ahem. We bullfrogs know where you can find some converters.
The bun-fairies are happy to assist where we can, as well.
I'll be watching you, though!
I don't...know what to say. Thank you.

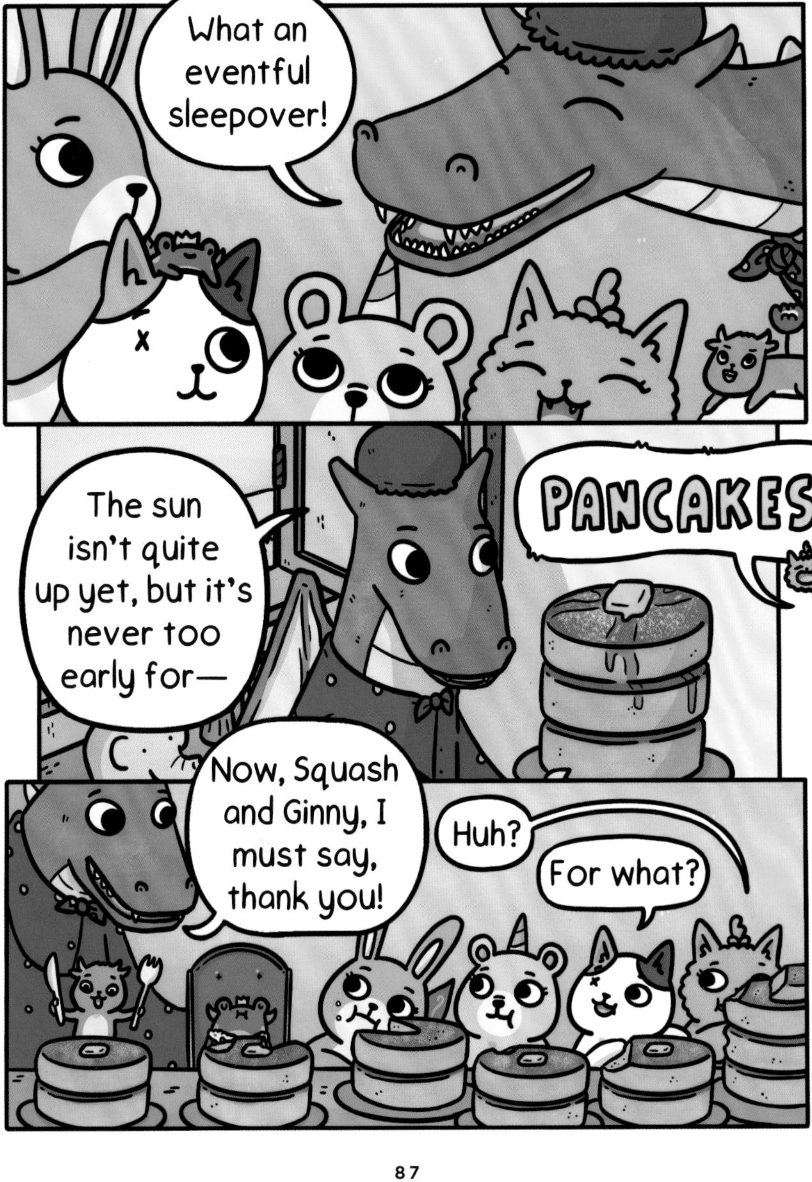
What an eventful sleepover!
The sun isn't quite up yet, but it's never too early for—
PANCAKES!
Now, Squash and Ginny, I must say, thank you!
Huh?
For what?

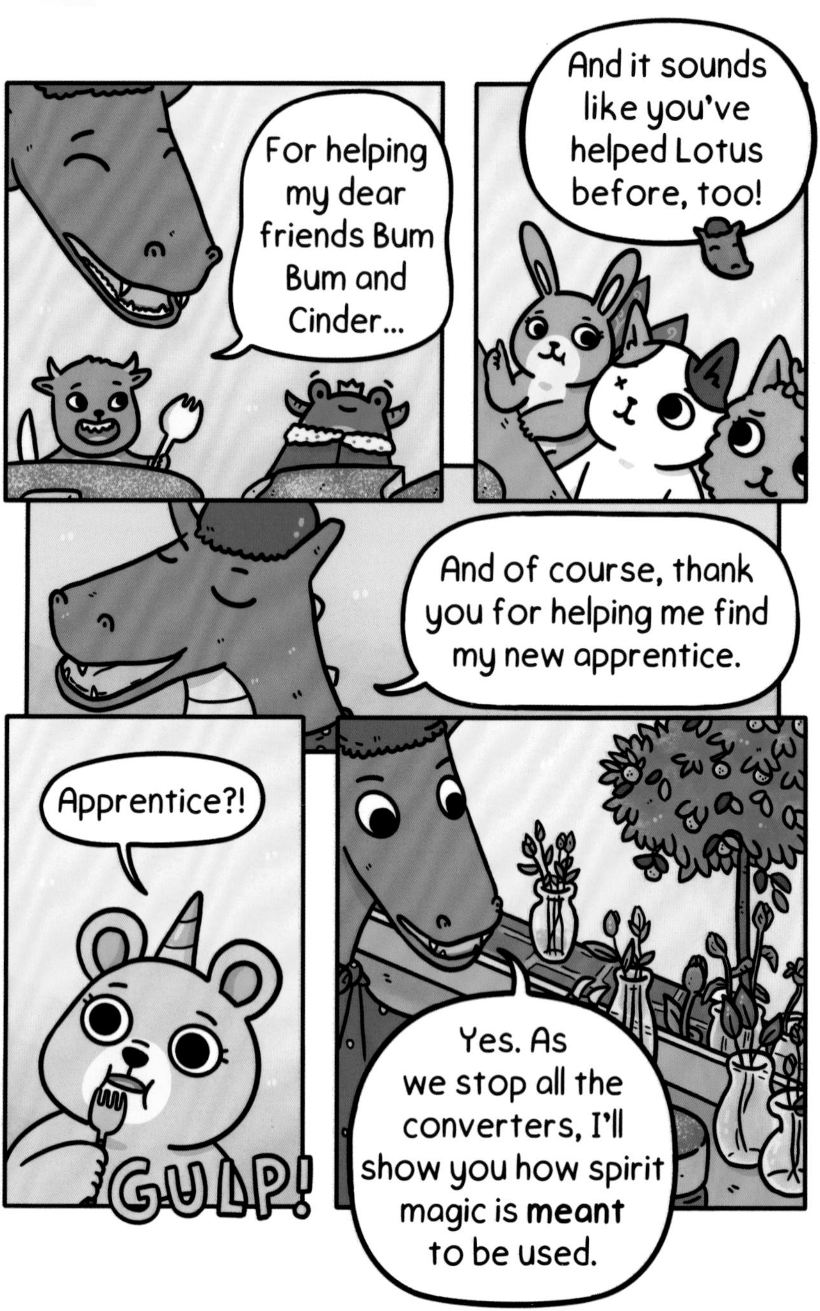
For helping my dear friends Bum Bum and Cinder...
And it sounds like you've helped Lotus before, too!
And of course, thank you for helping me find my new apprentice.
Apprentice?!
GULP!
Yes. As we stop all the converters, I'll show you how spirit magic is **meant** to be used.

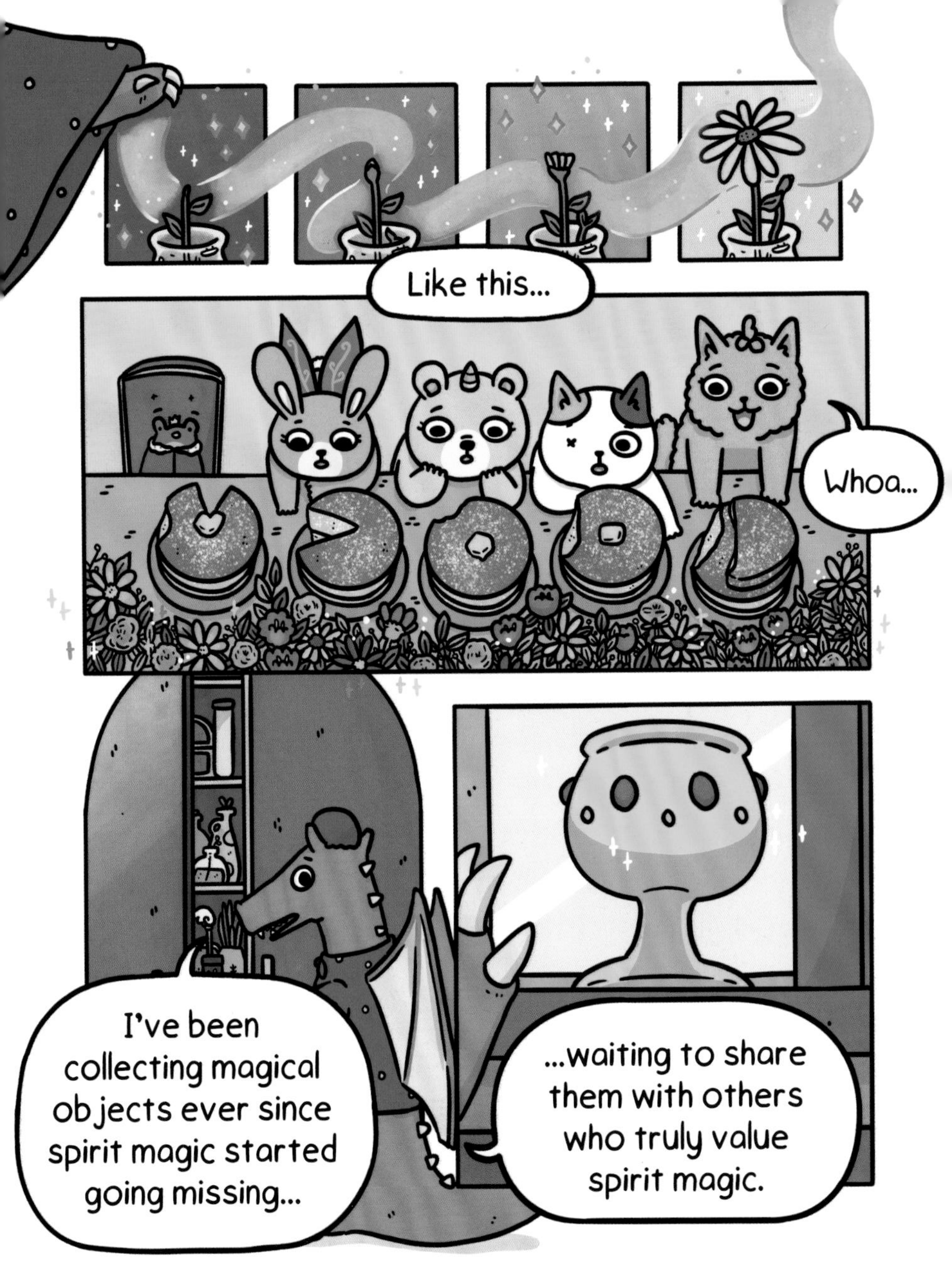
Like this...
Whoa...
I've been collecting magical objects ever since spirit magic started going missing...
...waiting to share them with others who truly value spirit magic.

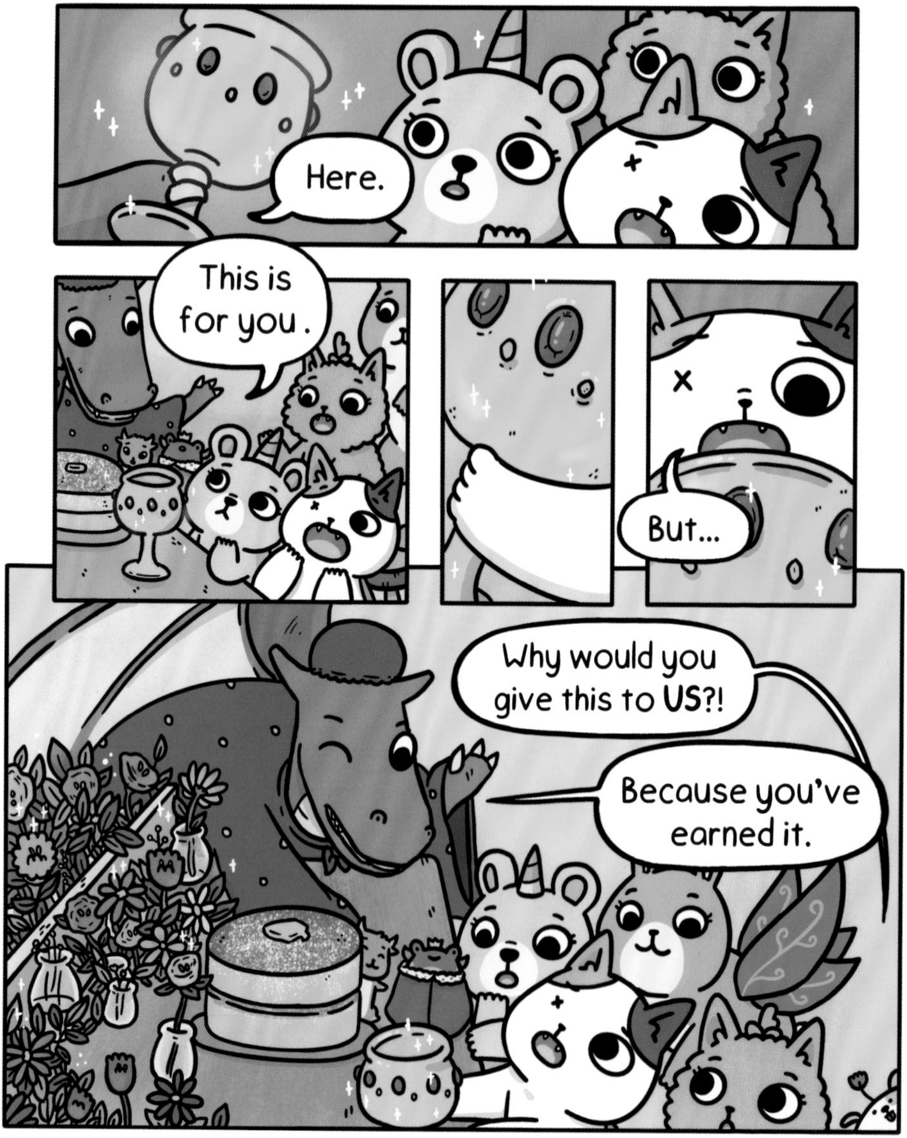
Here.
This is for you.
But...
Why would you give this to US?!
Because you've earned it.

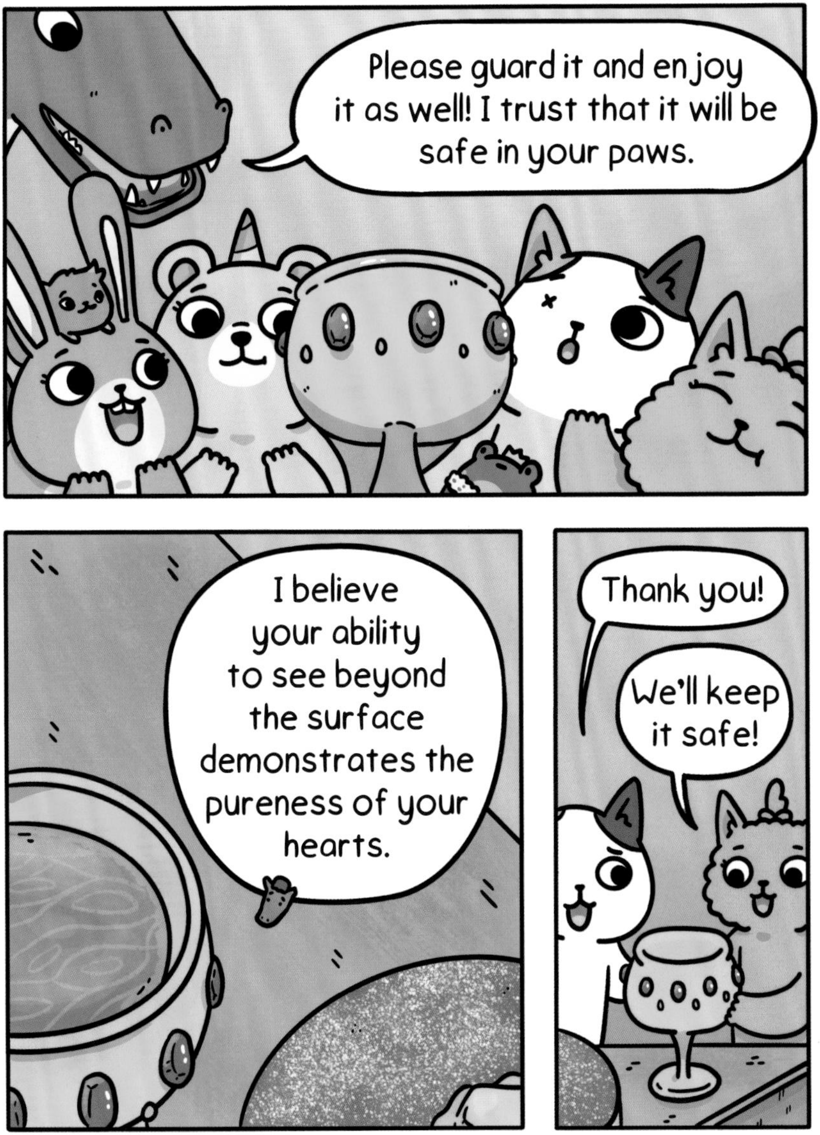
Please guard it and enjoy it as well! I trust that it will be safe in your paws.
I believe your ability to see beyond the surface demonstrates the pureness of your hearts.
Thank you!
We'll keep it safe!

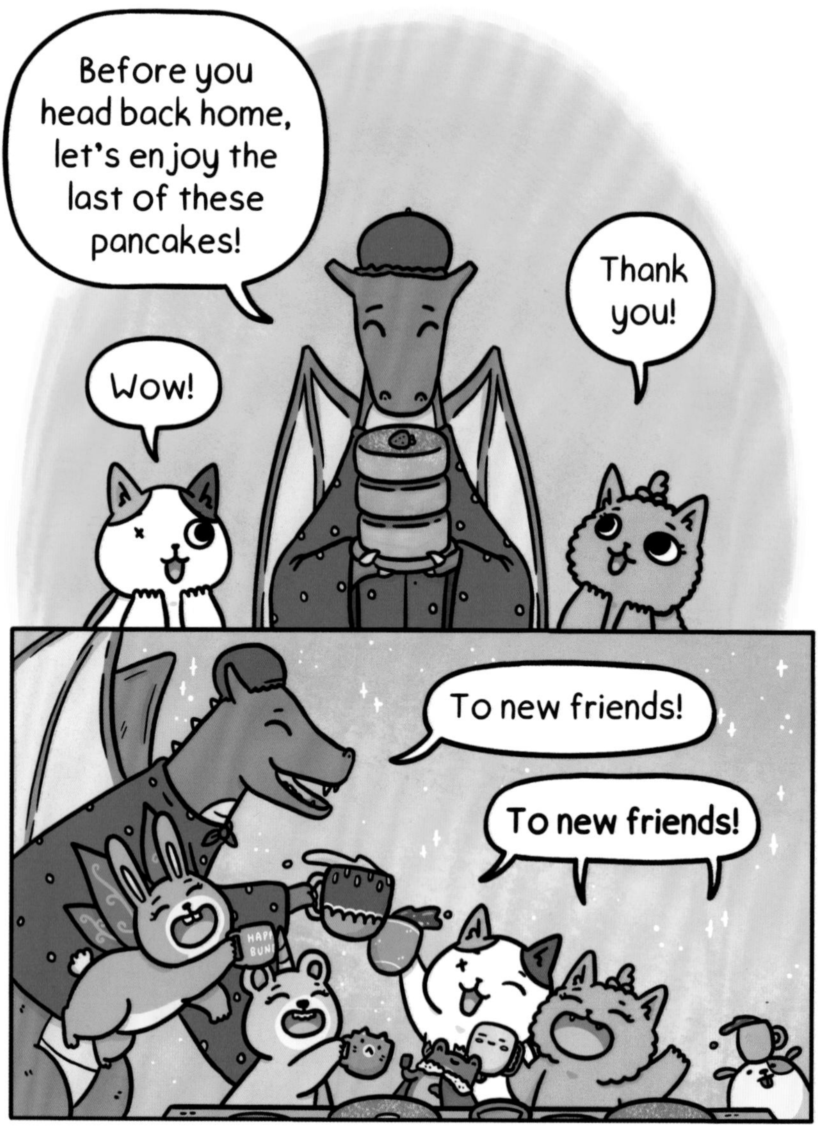

Before you head back home, let's enjoy the last of these pancakes!
Wow!
Thank you!
To new friends!
To new friends!
HAPPY BUN

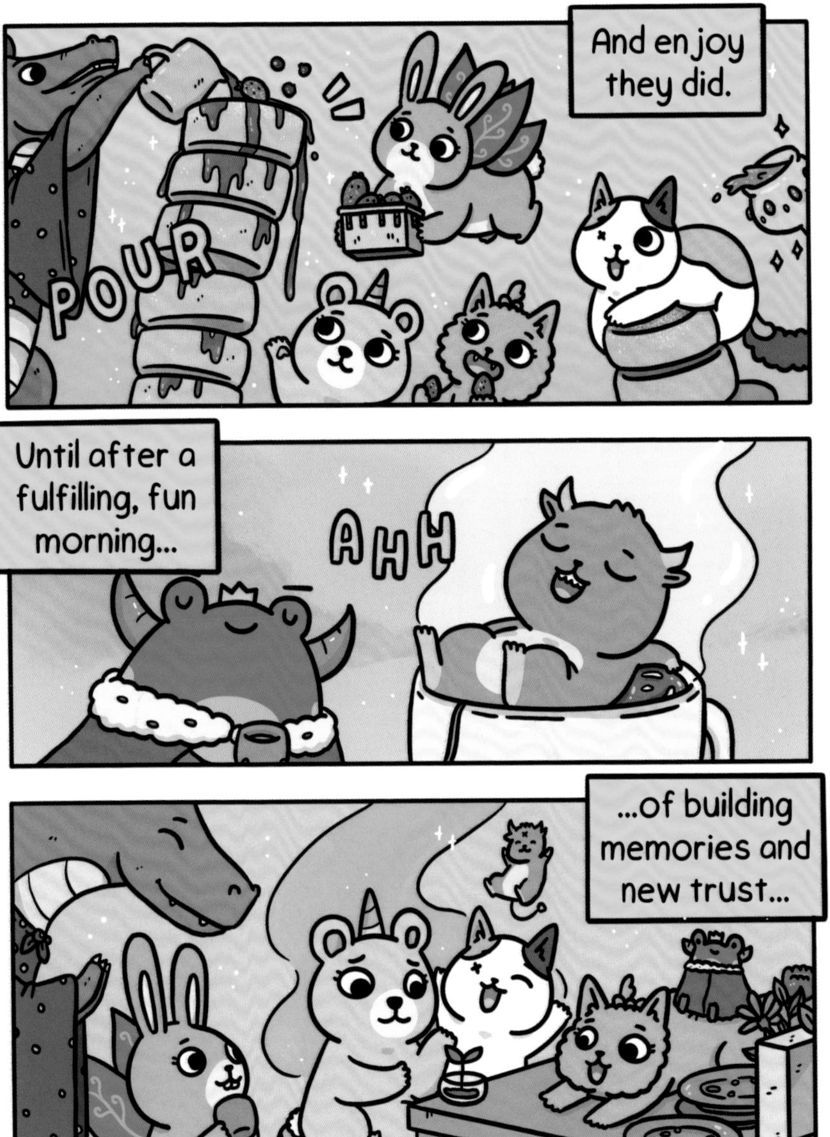
And enjoy they did.
POUR
Until after a fulfilling, fun morning...
AHH
...of building memories and new trust...

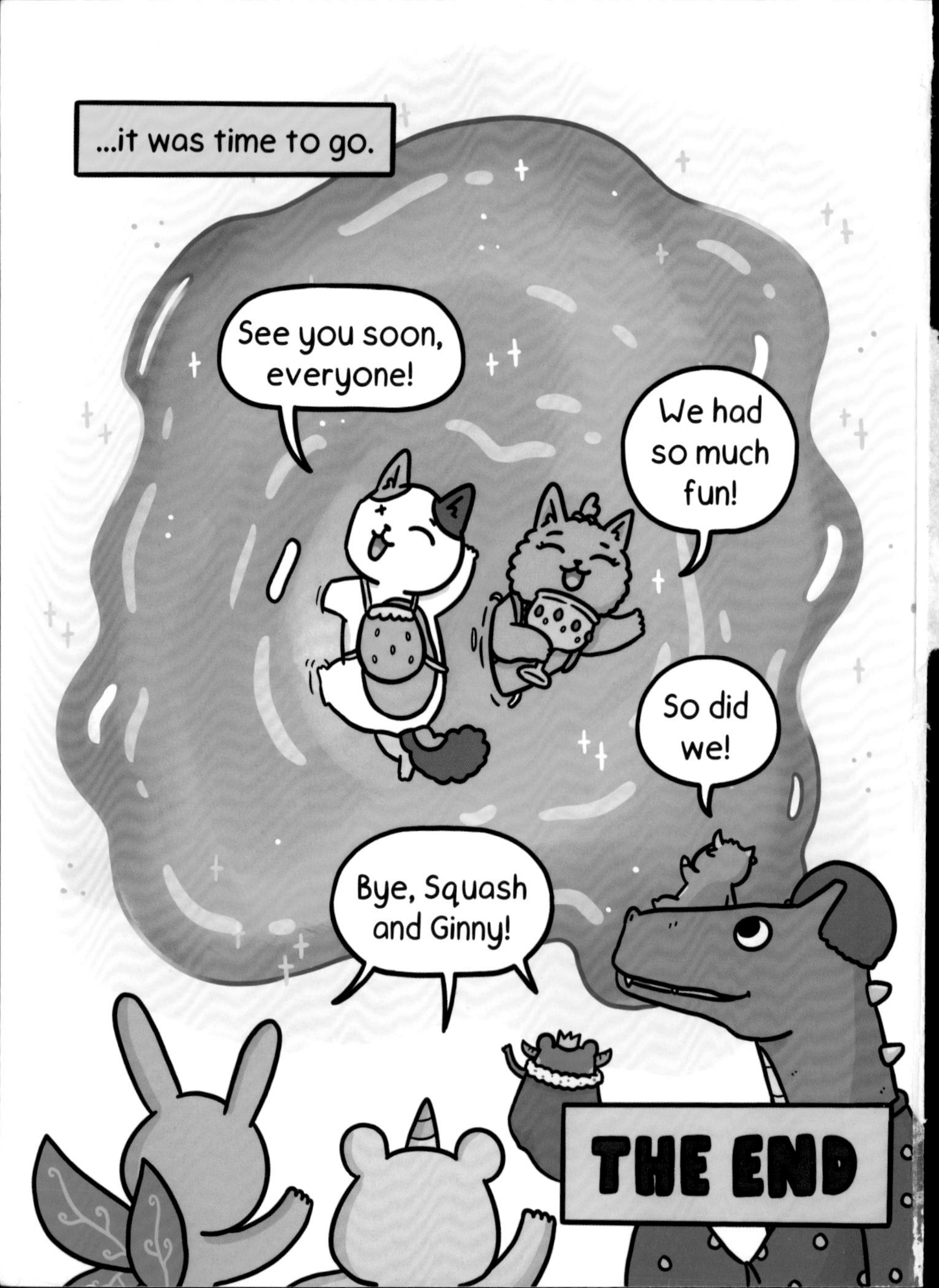
...it was time to go.
See you soon, everyone!
We had so much fun!
So did we!
Bye, Squash and Ginny!
THE END